THE DOOR TO FOREVER

DOUG SIMPSON

The Door to Forever is dedicated to those rare parents who understand that their children's invisible friends are not imaginary.

ACKNOWLEDGMENTS

A big thank you goes out to the Next Chapter team for their dedication and support for The Door to Forever.

1

Hi! My name is John. Just John will do. I am an old man now. I should've sat down decades ago and started writing this story, but I didn't. You know how life gets in the way of plans sometimes, right? Well, I am finally doing it even though this story never really ends because I am living it every time I wake up in the morning. If you are reading this, then you know I finished as much of the story as I could before I packed my bags for my final journey to Heaven.

It all began a long, long, long time ago. I think I was probably around four, maybe five. I had not started school yet. In my day, we did not have kindergarten, so we started school at age six.

My bedroom was also my playroom. Mom did not want my toys all over the house, so I spent a whole truckload of time in my bedroom, alone, or so I thought, anyway. One day this kid, a boy, showed up in my bedroom. Mom did not bring him in, I know that. At least I did not see her bring him in, and the way she acted later on when she found out about him pretty much confirmed that assertion. Of course, I cannot remember exact conversations from way back then, so I will simply create conversations based on the memories I have of those times. Some but not all of the names I do reveal are real, though.

"Hi, I'm Jason," he said.

"Hi."

"I came to play with you today. Is that okay?"

"Sure." I did not have a lot of friends when I was young. We lived out in the country where neighbors were pretty scarce, so I sure as heck was not going to say no to this welcome visitor, wherever he came from. He was a little taller than me but seemed to be around my age. "What would you like to play?"

"This is your house. What would you like to play?"

"I like to play war. I have lots of toy soldiers and army trucks. We can have lots of battles."

"Okay, let's play war, then."

We played war for a while and then I think we moved on to play farm. I also had lots of animals in my farm set, and I loved to put up fences to keep them from getting away. Jason and I enjoyed a great time playing together. It was wonderful to finally have a friend my age who liked the same toys that I did.

My mom startled me when she opened the bedroom door. "Lunchtime, John."

"Okay, Mom. Is Jason staying for lunch?"

"Who is Jason?" my mother asked with a strange look on her face.

"Jason, here," I replied and looked over to where I had last seen him, but he was gone. I looked all around the room to see where he was hiding.

"What are you doing now?" Mom asked, somewhat perturbed.

"Looking for Jason. He was right here."

"Come on, John. The soup is getting cold. Let's go. If Jason comes back, he can stay for lunch."

"Good. I like him."

Jason did not come back for lunch.

After lunch, I was eager to get back to my bedroom to see if Jason was hiding there somewhere. I did not see him at first and was disappointed, but then he reappeared behind me. "Where did you go?" I asked.

"I was here."

"Why didn't you come for lunch?"

"Your mom doesn't know me."

I found that a bit confusing, I think, but at the age of four or five, I did not really give it much thought. I was just thrilled that my new playmate was back or had not left. We had another great time playing for a couple of hours, and then Mom came into my room once again.

"Are you going to have an afternoon nap?"

"I am not tired, Mommy. I want to keep playing with Jason."

Mom carefully looked around my room for Jason, who, unfortunately for me, disappeared again. She glared at me for a few seconds then walked over and picked me up. She plunked me unceremoniously down on my bed and sat beside me. "It is not nice when you make up stories. Mommy does not like that."

"I am not making up stories, Mommy."

"Oh! Then where is Jason?"

"I don't know. He goes away when you come in the room."

"I see." Mom paused for a few moments as if she was uncertain what her next move should be. "Okay, listen to me carefully. I do not want to hear you talk any more about Jason. Do you understand?"

"Yes, Mommy."

3

"Good, now close your eyes and have a nap," she ordered and left the room.

It is difficult for me to remember all of the details from that day many years ago. I know I could not understand why Mommy was so upset about my new playmate, why she could not see him, and why Jason up and disappeared when she entered my room. I was trying to process all of this through my young mind when Jason walked up beside my bed.

"Hi, Johnny."

"Hi, Jason. Why do you go away when my mom comes into the room?"

"As you can see, she does not understand that I am really here."

"How come?"

"It's a bit hard for you to understand, I know. Just think of it as kind of like magic, okay."

"Okay. Mommy does not want me to play with you anymore."

"Johnny, she did not say that. She said she did not want you to talk to her about me anymore, right?"

I thought about that for a moment of two. "Yes, that's right. So, does that mean you will still come to play with me?"

"Yes, if you want me to."

"I want you to. I had lots of fun today playing with you."

"I had lots of fun, too. Just try and remember not to tell your mother or father that you were playing with me so you do not get them upset with you, okay?"

"Okay."

"Good. I am going to go away again and come back another day to play with you. You better take a nap like your mother told you so she is not upset with you again, okay?"

"Okay."

"Now close your eyes."

I closed my eyes for a little while and then peeked a few minutes later. Jason was gone.

Jason came back to play with me often. Not every day, but often. I had a great time playing with him. A while later, it was probably months later, I can't be sure, but I know it was not years later, he surprised me.

"Would it be okay if I bring some other friends along to play with us when I come back next time?"

"I guess so," I replied.

By that time spring had arrived, and since we lived out in the country and our house was a long ways from the road, I was allowed to play outside by myself. Jason had already begun to come and play with me while I was outside, as well as other times while I was up in my room.

The next day, I think, or at least soon after, Jason arrived with another boy and two girls. They appeared to all be around my age. I did not see where they came from; they just were there while I was playing by myself. Jason introduced his friends to me. The boy was called Tommy and the girls were Crystal and Nancy.

Our property had an old barn on it, and we had lots of fun playing hide and seek, climbing around the different levels of the barn and playing in the loose straw. From that day on Tommy, Crystal and Nancy pretty much always came along with Jason when he visited me. It was the best summer of my short life, without a doubt.

Approximately a year later, I think, one day in the fall, Jason called me aside when the five of us were playing in the barn.

"Let's go outside for a walk, just you and I. I have something I need to tell you."

The others continued to play in the barn while Jason and I walked along the path that ran away from the barn and house towards the back of the farm property. Jason was quiet for a few minutes, and then he stopped suddenly.

"I need to tell you something," he said after I stopped and faced him. "Pretty soon, probably in a month or so, I likely will not be able to come and play with you anymore, Johnny."

I burst into tears. "Why?" I blubbered between sobs. You are my best friend."

"I know, and I am sorry about this, but there is something else that I most likely will be required to do. If this event takes place, then I simply can't come and play with you anymore. The others will still come to play with you, but I likely will not be able to come much longer. Please don't cry."

About a month later, my mother delivered a healthy baby boy. She called him Jason.

Baby Jason was a hoot! I adored him the first time I set eyes on him. Of course, he did not look at all like my playmate Jason, except when we looked into each other's eyes. I was only six when he was born, but something in my heart told me that my two Jasons were really one. Baby Jason and I became best buddies immediately. Every time he saw me, his eyes lit up, and every time I saw him, my heart skipped a beat. Seventy-plus years later we are still good buddies, but unfortunately, after he grew up, he found his ideal job a couple hundred miles away from home, so we do not see each other often enough. The experiences I had in my later years, which you will hear about down the road, have left no doubt in my mind that my two Jasons are in fact one.

2

Tommy, Crystal and Nancy continued to visit me for play days, often. I missed having Jason to play with for sure, but the fact that I believed my two Jasons were really one made his loss easier to accept. As the weeks went by and winter approached, the four of us had many fun times together playing outside.

Before the first snowfall of the season, Crystal called me aside one day and pulled a Jason on me.

"I know it has only been a few months since Jason told you he would not likely be able to come and play with you much longer. Well, now it is my turn. Just like Jason, I must go off and do something else important in a month or so."

I didn't cry this time. It was not that I didn't like Crystal. The truth is that she was now my favorite playmate of the three, and I hated to hear that she too was going to leave me. "Are you going to end up in a new baby like Jason did?"

"How do you know about that?"

"The first time I stared into the eyes of my baby brother, Jason, my heart told me that he was really my playmate, Jason. I have no way to prove it; I just feel it in my heart."

Crystal smiled. "Your heart knows. You are still too young to understand how all of this works, but to answer your question, yes, I am going to end up in a new baby."

"How do you and Jason know so much about all of this when you cannot tell me the whole story?"

"When Jason, Tommy, Nancy and I are here playing with you, we do not have bodies like yours. We are just able to make ourselves look like children your age. That is why your mother and father cannot see us when we are playing. When we do not have bodies like you, we know way more than children your age, who are in bodies, know. When you get older, you will be able to understand this better, okay?"

"Okay, I guess."

About a month later, only Tommy and Nancy came to play.

For two years Tommy and Nancy were my regular playmates. They came more in the warmer months while I played outside than they did through the colder or stormy days when I spent more time indoors. They did occasionally join me in my bedroom/toy room, but we were careful to not play any noisy games where I might get excited and shout or say things that would cause my mother, in particular - as she was home most of the time – to investigate why I was causing a ruckus. After my mother had warned me back when I was four or five that she did not want to hear me talk about the disappearing Jason anymore, I obeyed her command and never, for a long time, mentioned my pop-in, pop-out playmates.

It would be approximately two years after Crystal disappeared from my playground that Nancy added herself to my missing playmates list. She did not do it when the two of us were alone but did it in front of Thomas as well.

"It is time for me to tell you that pretty soon I will no longer be coming around to play with you, Johnny."

My mother had revealed to Jason and me a few weeks

before that we were going to soon have a baby sister or brother, so Nancy's news was not exactly unexpected. "Are you going to become my sister?"

Nancy smiled. "Yes, that is the plan."

"Great. Will Mom call you Nancy?"

"That is up to your mother, but I know that Nancy is the name she has at the moment on the top of her list of names for this baby."

"Oh, how do you know that?"

"Just like how Tommy and I pop in to play with you at times, we can also pop in and see what is taking place anywhere inside your house, not just your bedroom. When we do that, we do not let anyone see us, so no one knows we are there, not even you."

"How does that work?"

"You are still not old enough to understand exactly what is going on. As you get older, Tommy will explain more and more about how this all works, trust me."

I turned to Tommy. "You're not going to disappear on me like the rest of them?"

"No. I am going to be with you for many, many years. I will be your guide, explaining, at the appropriate times, how all of our popping in and out works, as well as lots of other things that you have no idea about right now."

"Cool. How do you know all this?"

"That is one of the other things I will explain when you are older, okay?"

"Okay."

A few weeks later, our new sister arrived. Mom called her Nancy. As soon as we looked into each other's eyes, I knew my two Nancys were one. I'm sure she did also.

3

The years rolled by. I made friends at school, and Tommy visited me often, but never when anyone else was around. As I grew older, my curiosity about Tommy increased, and I would pepper him with questions at times. His usual response was that I was still not old enough to understand how he could pop into my world in a second or two and pop out just as quickly.

I graduated from elementary school. That meant a longer bus ride for high school to a larger, neighboring town than our local village. I am not naming many names in my story because I am writing this incognito, and I do not think I will end up revealing my real name. I'll just say that it is a writer's right to change his mind on that subject, so we shall see what we shall see as time passes and the story develops. High school brought to me an expanded collection of new friends. I enjoyed that immensely because growing up in the country at a young age resulted in my best friends being invisible to apparently everybody but me. Tom regularly popped in when convenient to my activities at home, and I was certainly always glad to see him. As I neared my teens, we agreed we should be called Tom and John instead of Tommy and Johnny.

I learned to drive when I was sixteen. I did not have my own car, so I could not toot around very much on my own. High school graduation brought on a new challenge. I had absolutely no inkling what I wanted to do with my life. My parents encouraged me to go on to college anyway and figure out my future during the journey. That reasoning kind of made sense to me, so that is precisely the approach I took. I chose a very reputable college in Cincinnati. It was approximately a two-hour drive from home, but a long walk. I still did not have a car at my disposal.

College life was fun, well, for a little while anyway. New friends, new school, big city, lots of drinking; what more could a teenager ask for? Unfortunately, it came to a crashing halt. It was five weeks after classes started. My roommate in the residence had a car, and we quickly bonded. We were out cruising for babes on a Saturday evening. We had a couple of beers, but we made sure we were not drunk. I heard squealing tires at an intersection, and then my lights went out.

The next thing I remember, I was in this luscious, strange place, sitting there under a tree chatting with my deceased grandfather. We were having a grand time reminiscing about the fun times we spent together while we were fishing the local lakes and streams. There were others there around us, but I cannot recall actually knowing any of them. Suddenly my grandfather looked up in the air, somewhere, and said, "You've got to go back." And then everything went blank.

Blank has no time, so it is difficult to say how long I was gone. Then, there I was back again, chatting with my beloved grandfather as if I had never left. It was a shorter chat this time, and then everything went blank again.

The next thing I remember, I was in a hospital room, surround by doctors, nurses, and my family. I was pretty much covered in bandages and medical tubes. My mother burst into happy tears when I opened my eyes and blankly stared around the room.

Before I continue with the story, I want to first go back and fill you in on the information I later discovered about the squealing tires and everything else that occurred before I woke up to the welcoming committee assembled in my hospital room.

My roommate and I were having a great time singing our hearts out to the song on the radio. I cannot remember what the song was anymore. We were going through an intersection with the right-of-way and another vehicle, driven by one of our own college students who apparently did not see his stop sign to the right of me, or our car, until the last second and slammed on his brakes. Unfortunately, not soon enough for me, and his car smashed into my door. That is when my lights went out, and I remember nothing until I was sitting up in the clouds enjoying my chat with my dearly departed grandfather.

I was in pretty bad shape. Actually, that is a bit of an understatement; I was in terrible shape. I had head injuries, internal injuries, a shattered right thigh bone, and a broken right arm below the elbow. Fortunately, the nearest hospital was only a couple of blocks away from our accident scene, so they had me in the emergency room within minutes. My roommate, as well as the driver of the other car and his passenger, only suffered minor injuries, so I was the top priority patient on arrival.

Because my lights were out, I cannot tell you everything that happened. I was told my heart stopped for seven minutes at one point in the operating room. That must have been when I paid my first visit to my grandfather. They got my heart going again, and obviously, my soul returned to my body, but I remember nothing from that time as my lights were still out. For some reason, my heart stopped another time, apparently for only a minute or two, and that was when I paid Grandpa a second but abbreviated visit.

I remember nothing from that point on until I woke up some thirty-six hours later in my hospital room. Even then, I was spaced out on pain killers and do not remember much. My mother told me many months later that the doctors had indicated that my chances of survival after they pieced me back together were a coin toss. Fortunately, the coin landed heads.

After the doctors assured my parents that I was out of danger and on my way to a slow recovery, my family returned back home but usually visited me on the weekends. My college roommate was my most common visitor, but a few other students that I became friendly with over my five weeks at college, as well as the driver of the car that smashed into us, dropped in occasionally. And let's not forget Tom. He may not count as a person, but he counts as a visitor.

I was in a semi-private room and, at times, had a roommate, but more often than not, I was the only resident. I had understood a long time before the accident that Tom could pop in and not be seen, or he could pop in and be seen only by me. He told me he checked in on me many times each day, but only made himself visible when things were pretty quiet around there, and we were not likely to be disturbed by an unexpected visitor or nurse. Even though all or most other people could not see him, he figured it would not look too good if a nurse or doctor checked in on me and caught me talking away to nobody. It was difficult for me to disagree with Tom on that one.

When we had time to chat, I told Tom about my visits with my grandfather. He assured me that those visits were not imaginary but real. When my heart stopped pumping, my soul departed from my body and visited with the soul of my grandfather on the other side. This was not at all unusual, according to Tom, but most people, like even me, he mentioned, do not talk about it after it happens because they feel that others will think their head injuries rattled their sanity. Fortunately for me, I guess, my earlier experiences with Jason, Crystal, Nancy, and Tom prepared me to readily accept that I did indeed have an enjoyable but brief visit with my dearly departed Grandpa.

Now that I was more or less grown up and experienced my first trips to Heaven, Tom was ready to fill me in a little on how all of this worked. He explained that on the death of a body, the soul and spirit depart and travel to the other side, or Heaven if you prefer the term. Souls there can then assume a variety of responsibilities during their tenure on the other side, just like he was my guide through the previous ten years or so, and Jason, Crystal, and Nancy were my playmates for a shorter while, before their next incarnation in a new body. There were oodles of other responsibilities that souls on the other side could assume, but that chat would take place down the road sometime, Tom advised me.

I was not allowed to get out of bed for three months because of the condition of my shattered thigh bone. Then, they fitted me with a cast, but not a walking cast, for another month. It was wonderful to be able to just hobble around the hospital a bit on my crutches and see more of the world I desperately missed. I next got a walking cast for a couple of more months. When it was removed, I experienced the tortures of rehab therapy. Not fun, but necessary.

I, of course, missed the remainder of my first year of college. Five weeks of classes does not qualify for any credits. The good news was that I was allowed to return home to my parents for the summer as long as I promised to continue my therapy exercises. That was a pleasure, I assure you. Being home, I mean, not the therapy exercises.

4

E very morning, early before it got too hot, and every
evening as the sun was setting, I made it a habit,
except on stormy days, to walk out to the rear of the
farm, and back again of course. Very seldom on the morning
jaunts but more often in the evenings, Jason or Nancy, or
sometimes both of them, would accompany me. It was good
exercise for all of us.

On the jaunts when I was alone, Tom sometimes popped
in to accompany me. Because of my experiences visiting with
Grandpa in Heaven, along with Tom's explanations of those
visits, I believed I was ready to hear further explanations
concerning how all of this worked. Tom agreed, to a point, so
he answered some of my questions and deferred others to his
famous 'later.'

"Jason, in spirit form, visited me first when I was probably
almost five, and then not too long after that initial visit, he
brought along you, Nancy, and Crystal to play with me,
right?"

"Right," Tom said.

"You told me you would not be disappearing as my playmate like the others did, and you were remaining as my guide, right?"

"Right."

"So, are you what is referred to in books as my Spirit Guide for this incarnation?"

"That's me."

"Figured as much. So, you don't get to pop into bodies like the others have done?"

"Not this time around, or in proper terminology, not in this round of incarnations."

"Explain, please."

"You, I, Nancy, Jason, Crystal, your parents, your grand-parents, Crystal's parents and grandparents, and many, many others are currently part of the same soul group. The souls in a soul group reincarnate together throughout a number of different time periods, sometimes hundreds of years apart. They are seldom in the same relationship as they were in their previous incarnations, but they also could be. For example, in your previous incarnation, your grandpa might have been your son or brother, or even your mother or sister. Souls are sexless. It is the human bodies that are male and female. Most souls will experience lives as males at times and females at other times. They will also experience incarnations in different cultures, different races, different religions, and different geographical regions. I know that is a lot to digest at once, but you wanted more information. Now I hope you also understand why I could not tell you about this when you were younger, and I probably would not be telling you even now at nineteen either if it had not been for your soul's vivid visits with your grandfather."

"Wow! That definitely is a lot to digest."

"Yep. I will stop there and let you think about all of this for quite some time before we take it to the next level."

"Okay. That makes good sense to me."

Now and then I would ask Tom about certain aspects of his explanations, but I never hounded him to go on to anything new. "Do you also visit with Jason, Nancy, and Crystal?" I asked one day on our walk together.

"I check up on them but do not visit in the same way I visit with you."

"So, you are not their Spirit Guide also?"

"No. Everyone has their own Spirit Guide. There are also other spirits that assist different people with specialized problems or situations."

"Explain, please."

"I am your Spirit Guide for day-to-day living. If you had a tough problem, say, in mechanics or aeronautics, then another guide, expert in those fields, would try to help you with these unique areas. Think of me as a generalist in your soul group. Make sense?"

"Yes, but you also said you looked in on Jason, Nancy, and Crystal."

"I pop in and check up on them often, but they do not see me, just like I pop in and check on your mom and dad also. We are all part of the same soul group, remember?"

"I understand. So, you know where Crystal is?"

"Yes."

"Where is she?"

"She is not too far away."

"But where?"

"I cannot tell you."

"Why."

"Her information is private to her, not just anyone who wants to know. Because you two are in our soul group, then someday your paths may cross again. Humans have free will to make decisions in their lives. Let me explain it this way. If you decided to go to college in Chicago, you would not have been in your accident in Cincinnati."

"You mean I would not have been in an accident at all?"

"I didn't say that. You could not have been in the accident in Cincinnati if you were in Chicago. We will never know if you would have been in an accident in Chicago because you were not there. Think of life as a journey of many choices. Your choices create certain possibilities and eliminate others. Make sense?"

"Kind of."

Changing topics on you, readers, but not time frames, when I came home from the hospital after rehab, I wanted to find a summer job to earn some money. My father put the kibosh on that very quickly. He insisted that my primary concern was my health. He also added that money was not going to be a problem anymore. After the accident, he had quickly contacted his lawyer who referred him to a very successful personal injury lawyer. It also turned out that the father of the other driver was a big company executive with oodles of money and insurance coverage. There was not going to be a big legal battle over a reasonable settlement. The main obstacle to an early settlement was waiting for my recovery to see the extent of any permanent disabilities I might have. Fortunately, the only long-term problem has been arthritis in my shattered thigh bone.

The driver's father visited my parents at home one day just before I was released from the hospital. He told them that he would pay for all of my educational expenses, including residence fees, as long as I continued attending college or university, and that this was in addition to the settlement arranged between the insurance company and our lawyer. He only asked that this be our secret and not shared with the insurance company or our lawyer. Of course, we agreed. The driver's father kept his promise one hundred percent.

The insurance company and our lawyer settled my injury compensation just before Christmas. Marvelous timing! I paid off the mortgage on my parents' farm, in spite of their protests, bought myself a fairly new Chevy Impala, and banked the rest for future reference. For the first time, I joined the happy minority of students with their own vehicle at college. The unfortunate accident taught me a life-changing lesson. I buckled down and became a nerdy student. I also made sure my alcohol intake was restricted to a bare minimum.

My Chevy Impala made me popular with the ladies, but I was careful to avoid the party babes. I dated the bookworms instead. No regrets. I enjoyed the company of a number of girlfriends over my college years, but none of these relationships felt like they should be made permanent.

5

Time flies by when we are not paying attention. I graduated from university with a Master's Degree in English Literature. I also obtained my secondary school teacher's license. There was no teacher surplus back when I was getting into the profession, but there were a lot of qualified and experienced English teachers. I enjoyed my college years in Cincinnati, but I was definitely a country boy at heart. I tried extensively to snag an English teacher's position in the smaller secondary schools in the quieter towns but was not successful, so I grudgingly settled for one in Cincinnati.

I was pretty sure that after I had a few years of teaching under my belt that I would be successful in obtaining a position in a more laidback environment. I was right. After three years of teaching in the city, I was hired for a vacant position in the high school I graduated from ten years earlier. If that was not unusual enough, the English Department Head in the school had been my English teacher in my senior years. It definitely brings destiny to my mind.

The only hitch was that the vacancy was officially a one-year replacement for a teacher going on a maternity leave. The principal and the English Head both emphasized that they were almost certain the pregnant lady, they both knew quite well, was planning to stay home until her child was old enough to attend school. But, for the record, she requested a one-year leave. I knew it was a gamble, but I wanted to teach in my old school, so I took a chance. I won. The new mother resigned her position a year later, and it was officially mine. It gets even better. I moved back into my bedroom at my parent's farmhouse, with their encouragement. My brother and sister had also moved out, so my folks were happy for the company, and I figured I was handy to take care of them if needed as they aged.

I guess it is not really a digression if I go back to my brother and sister. Jason had been recently hired by the Kentucky State Police as an in-car patrolman. Nancy was studying art in France and living with a Frenchman, fellow artist.

I was happy teaching in my former high school and living at home. Two years passed with minimum excitement. I dated some very nice young women over that period, but none of them registered as my once-in-a-lifetime partner. Our home life received a bit of a shakeup in the summer after my second year back home.

Just a reminder, readers. I hoped to be able to avoid mentioning many names I wished to keep secret, but it is turning out to be basically impossible, so I came up with a compromise. I have substituted fictitious names for actual family and town names from time to time.

"John," my mother hollered out the back door as I was sitting in the shade before lunch, reading one of the books I was scheduled to teach in English class in a few weeks. "Roger is on the phone for you."

The only Roger I could think of was the Principal of our

high school, so I hustled inside to see what he was up to. "Good morning, Roger."

"Good morning, John. Sorry to interrupt your holidays but I have a little problem I hope you can help me with. I am sitting here in my office opposite a very bright young lady who I would love to hire for our current, vacant English position, but she has a geography problem we must solve first. She is from out of town, does not drive, and has been searching all around Promenade for two days for a furnished apartment to rent, or even a room in a nice home. I know you would not mind driving her into school with you if she was able to find a place to rent there in your vicinity. Do you have any ideas at all of places she could rent along your route to school?"

"Hang on a minute, Roger. I want to ask my mother, and she is out in the kitchen right now." I hurried out to the kitchen and explained the situation to my mother. "Roger seems pretty keen on grabbing this young lady. Would you and Dad be okay with letting her move into Nancy's room for a while?"

Mom thought the situation over for maybe fifteen seconds. "That's fine. Tell Roger she has a place to live and to sign her up."

"Thanks, Mom." I hustled back to the telephone, the only telephone on the first floor in those days. "Sign her up, Roger. My brother and sister have moved away, and it is only my parents and I here in this big old farmhouse. She can move into my sister's former room and drive to school with me. How did she get to the school?"

"Her parents have been here with her all along."

"Good. If she is happy with our offer, finish up your paperwork, then call me back so we can arrange for them to meet me out here in Mantle, so they can follow me to our house. That will probably be an easier way for them to get here than me giving them all of the different turns they would be required to make if they tried it on their own." I should add, for you readers, that this was way before GPS systems were invented.

"Thank your mother for us. I am sure our new teacher will be thrilled. I'll call again when they are ready to go out there."

I went outside to retrieve the book I was reading and parked myself on the sofa in the living room next to the telephone. It rang in less than a half an hour.

"Hello."

"Hi, John. It's a done deal. I'm sure we have us a crackerjack new English teacher on our hands. Her parents are here in the office with us, so the three of them are eager to make arrangements to meet you and your mother, as well as see our young lady's new residence. It is almost lunchtime, so they would like to go out for lunch here to celebrate the good news and would prefer to meet you after lunch in Mantle, when convenient for you."

"That makes good sense. They know how to get to Mantle?"

"Yes. It is on those backroads that they are more likely to get lost."

"How about we meet on Main Street, in front of the Post Office, at one-thirty?"

Roger checked with his visitors. "That works for them. How will they recognize you?"

"I pretty much know everyone in Mantle. If they stand in front of the Post Office, it will not be difficult for me to pick out three strangers with wide grins on their faces."

Roger could not catch his laugh before it escaped. "Cute! I'll share that one with them. They are Crystal, Cassandra, and Martin Wilson."

I immediately twigged to the name, Crystal, but of course, I could not be sure if Crystal was the mother or the daughter. I had known a few Crystals at college, and even dated one, but

I never had the gut feeling that any of them was the spirit Crystal who visited me for one summer when I was five. I also remembered that when the spirit Nancy told me, in response to my question, that she would become my sister Nancy, but it was my mother's decision which name she chose for my sister. Even though Nancy was the name on the top of my mother's list of names for a girl, she could always change her mind before the official naming. That would mean, I figured, that my spirit Crystal might not even be called Crystal today, so I was determined to not prematurely get my hopes up once again.

I was waiting in front of the Post Office in Mantle by one-fifteen. No strangers were in sight, so I remained in my car for ten minutes or so until two women and a man I did not recognize came hustling down the sidewalk towards the Post Office. When they stopped directly in front of the Post Office and looked around the neighborhood, I got out of the car and walked over towards them. "Hi, I'm John. Are you folks the Wilsons?" They were, of course, and they followed me along the rural roads to our farm.

Mom was eagerly waiting for us and spotted the cars coming along the gravel driveway long before we reached the house. She welcomed our visitors heartily and gave them a quick tour of the first floor before taking them upstairs to Nancy's old room. "This was our daughter's room. She loved pink and white, which is obvious when you look around, and it will be your room, Crystal. What do you think?"

"It will be wonderful. Thank you so much for opening your home to me, a total stranger, Mrs. Tranter."

"You are most welcome. Roger was thrilled with you, so I hear, and you will be working with John, so this arrangement makes perfect sense to me."

"How long will she be able to stay here?" Cassandra asked.

Mom paused for a few seconds as if she never even

thought about that question. "Crystal is welcome to stay as long as she wants or needs to. It is totally up to her."

"Oh, thank you, Mrs. Tranter," Crystal said and gave my mother a long hug.

"It is nothing," Mom responded, obviously blushing. "Come; let's quickly check out the other rooms up here. Then we can go downstairs to the living room and get better acquainted. I also have a fresh pot of tea waiting for us along with some carrot cake."

Everyone chatted over refreshments for a half an hour, and when there was a lull in the conversation, I stood up. "If you folks would excuse us for a few minutes, I would like to take Crystal outside and show her around the property."

"Go ahead, kids," Cassandra responded. "It will give us an opportunity to tell tales about you two when you are gone," she teased.

"Mother!" Crystal said somewhat loudly as she stood up and placed her hands on her hips. "Don't you dare!"

Everyone had a good laugh as I led Crystal out the back door to the yard. I took her on a bit of a circular pattern so she could see the far side of the house, then we continued along the edge of the cornfield behind the yard, towards the barn and the laneway, which is actually an extension of the driveway. "Every morning at sunrise, except school days and during bad weather, and every evening before sunset, weather permitting, I like to walk out to the rear of the farm. I think I have been doing this since possibly before I started elementary school. Sometimes my brother or sister or both would accompany me after they got old enough. If you like fresh air and long walks you are welcome to join me on these excursions after you move in with us. No pressure, of course, but I just wanted to point out that you are welcome to do so."

"Thank you, John. I would love to join you on your walks."

"Wonderful. Come, and I will show you inside the old

barn. We do not farm the land here ourselves. It is rented out to a neighbor and has been for a couple of decades or more. I used to spend many hours playing in the old barn when I was young, and so did my brother and sister when they were old enough. Even when we were kids, there was no farm equipment in the barn, just lots and lots of loose straw. The farmer who rents the land takes his equipment home as he farms a number of neighboring properties as well. My dad and I use the barn in the bad weather to park our cars in." I slid open one of the doors and allowed Crystal to enter first.

She walked to the center of the barn and stood there, slowly turning in circles for at least a minute or two. "I know I have never been here before, but for some strange reason I feel like I recognize the inside of this barn," she said and looked at me.

Her words caused a happy smile to break out on my face.

"What is so funny?" she asked when she spotted my grin.

Oh boy! How do I get out of this one without lying to her, I wondered, or even worse, telling her the truth and have her think I was absolutely bonkers. "I was happy to hear your words," I offered as a response, hoping she would be satisfied with that.

"I do not understand why my words would thrill you so much."

I bit my lip and tried to come up with an answer that would satisfy her. "Yes, there is a special reason why I was so happy to hear what you said. Trust me, if I told you that reason right now, you would probably think I was a nut-case and run screaming back to the house. After you have moved in and realize I am not actually a nut-case at all, then, if you ask that question again, I will give you the truthful answer, okay?"

Crystal stared at me with a funny look, and I could tell she was trying to analyze the situation to determine her plan of action. "Okay," she sighed, "I am not going to forget about this and will hound you at some point until you spill the beans."

"It's a deal. I promise. When the time is right, I will tell you the absolute truth. Keep in mind that I could have lied to you about why I was smiling at your words, but that is not me. I hope you believe me."

She stared at me again for what felt like an eternity. "Okay, I believe you."

6

oger scheduled a meet-and-greet on the Friday morning before the school year started, with a barbeque lunch to follow. Cassandra and Martin transported Crystal and her belongings to our farmhouse on the previous morning, and as prearranged by my mother, they enjoyed lunch with Mom and me before leaving Crystal in our capable hands.

That first evening, as she indicated she would a few weeks earlier, Crystal joined me on my walk along the laneway to the rear of the farm. On our arrival back at the yard, she asked if we could go inside the barn again. I said of course, and I made it a point to assure her that as she was now a resident on our farm, she could venture anywhere at all that she wished to go. Inside, she once again morphed into a dreamy state as she slowly turned in a circle, checking all around the barn's interior. "I cannot for the love of me figure out why this barn seems so familiar. I also cannot wait to hear your explanation concerning why this makes you so happy," she said as she stared at my once-again-happy face.

"Soon. I only want you to better know the real me, and then I will share my secret with you."

With five years of experience under my belt, the beginning of the school year was no longer a big deal to me. Crystal, on the other hand, needed to learn everything from scratch. The first year or two of teaching is never easy, and she had many questions for me, but overall, I was delighted to watch her debut in the profession sail along rather smoothly.

We continued our evening walks, except in the bad weather, and snatched every opportunity for a morning walk that we could. I was a little surprised but definitely pleased, that Crystal always wanted to end each walk with another visit to the empty barn. Of course, I knew why she was drawn there, but if her subconscious mind ever fed her any clues as to what caused this attraction, she never shared it with me.

The conversations to and from school each day were primarily about school activities or problems, whereas while we were on our walks, I tried to keep our conversations on us, in an attempt to allow us to get to know more about each other. I never specifically mentioned this to Crystal, so if she brought up a school question, I dealt with it. The more time that we devoted to personal topics, the more I became enamored with this brilliant and beautiful young lady. At times I felt I sensed that she was also developing similar feelings towards me.

I remember one particular evening as if it were yesterday. It was the Friday of our third week of school. Throughout our walk, we both instigated a lot of playful teasing, resulting in much laughter and physical contact as we childishly pushed each other for making teasing comments. At the conclusion of this walk, Crystal took her usual detour into the barn. After her standard, slow, dreamy circle in the center of the barn, she did not stop as was her usual custom. She started doing beautiful pirouettes, gradually spinning closer and closer towards me until she stopped right in front of me, flashing a cheek-to-cheek grin.

"Where did you learn how to do that?"

"Ballet lessons and figure skating lessons."

"You are amazing, you know."

"I'm glad you think so."

"Would it be alright if I kissed you?"

"I only have one question. Why did it take you so long?" and without waiting for a reply, she stretched her arms around my neck and initiated our first kiss.

I reached around her waist and cemented our bodies together. Kiss after kiss after kiss followed each other with barely a break for a quick breath. At times it seemed like she was almost attempting to devour me. My hormones rocketed into overdrive, and my manhood reacted accordingly. I suspect she felt it dancing in my jeans against her thigh and she immediately broke loose stepping backwards.

"Wow! That was powerful! No one's kisses have ever affected me like that before," she panted. "I think my temperature must be at least a hundred and thirty. I need to go outside where the breeze is," she said, grabbing my hand and dragging me with her.

Outside, I watched with delight as she tried to fan herself with her hand and bring her panting under control at the same time. I waited patiently, unsure as to what was going to come next.

After her breathing returned close to normal, she stared at me. "I meant what I said. No guy has ever revved up my motor like that before. Unfortunately, it creates a problem that we need to talk about, now. I plan to save my virginity for my wedding night, so we cannot go any further than we did just now."

"That is wonderful. I admire you for that, so stick to your guns."

Crystal had a shocked look on her face. "That doesn't bother you?"

"No. I have had many different girlfriends over the past decade. Some were sexually active, and I readily admit I thoroughly enjoyed our hook-ups. I also had some girlfriends who, like you, wished to preserve their virginity for marriage, and I respected their wishes entirely. I do hope you will be my next girlfriend in a no-sex romance."

"You are absolutely amazing, my new boyfriend," she quietly said as she charged into my arms and initiated another series of explosive kisses.

It was almost dark. As we walked towards the house with our arms around each other, we agreed that we should keep our romance a secret from everyone except our two sets of parents. We walked into our living room hand in hand and, as I knew we would, shocked my parents into absolute silence. "Mom and Dad, I would like you to meet my new girlfriend, Crystal."

7

The next morning Crystal and I went for our usual walk, but our attitudes towards each other were now changed after the developments from the evening before. We walked hand in hand or sometimes with an arm around each other, and basically never lost physical contact with the other unless one of us decided to tickle the other, who then needed to escape temporarily. Keeping her record intact, Crystal headed into the barn when we returned to the backyard. She completed her dreamy circle as usual in the middle of the barn and then headed for the door. No kiss this time, but that was okay because I snuck a number of those in during our walk.

Crystal and I concentrated on school work for most of the morning and ate lunch with my mom and dad. I have not specifically mentioned it to you earlier, but Mom prepared the meals for all of us. Crystal and I were free to prepare other things on our own if we chose to do so. That was the arrangement Mom made with me when I moved back home years earlier, and she invited Crystal to operate the same way. It was hard to beat Mom's cooking, so we seldom did our own thing.

Crystal made a habit of helping Mom with the dishes whenever she was home, while generally Dad and I got to rest up in the living room. When the ladies were finished in the kitchen that day, I asked Mom if she could round me up an old, thick comforter or blanket that I could spread out up in the hayloft, which was still covered with old, loose straw. That is where I used to play often with my invisible friends, and that is where I wanted to reveal my secret to my new girlfriend.

"What do you want to go up there for?" Mom asked.

"That is where I used to spend so much time playing when I was young, and I am going to take Crystal up there for a little quiet relaxation."

Mom gave Crystal an inquiring look.

She smiled. "Don't worry, Mrs. Tranter. Nothing inappropriate is going to take place up there, trust me."

Mom grinned and took off in search of the requested comforter.

Inside the barn, I climbed up the ladder to the hayloft first so Crystal could see how easy it was. For the city folks reading this who have never been inside an old barn, I will digress momentarily and explain what these ladders looked like. Many old barns had these ladders constructed right up against a side or interior wall where they allowed a climber to get access to the hayloft. They were built strong to hold workers weighing well over two hundred pounds.

I laid out the old comforter on the straw near the center of the hayloft. There were still a few old bales of straw around, so I rounded up two of them and set them side by side at the edge of the comforter, so we could lean against them if we sat on the comforter or we could sit on them if we preferred. It also left a lot of room where we could stretch out side by side on the comforter whenever that was the preferred position. Crystal watched all of this in silence, so when I was finished, I sat down on the comforter and leaned against one straw bale.

"What in the world are we doing up here anyway?" Crystal asked.

"You have been curious for weeks about why I smile every time you wonder why the old barn seems familiar to you. Today I plan to solve the mystery for you. Make yourself comfortable wherever you like." She sat down beside me and leaned on her straw bale. "Before I begin, I need to ask you a question or two."

"Okay."

"Did you ever have invisible visitors as a child? You know, other children that you could see and play with but your parents could not see and did not believe existed."

Crystal grinned. God, what an adorable grin. My heart leapt, and I wanted to grab her and kiss her unmercifully, but that would have to wait. "Yes. I gather you did also?"

"Oh, yes. I want to hear all about your visitors, but it is best if I tell you about my experiences first, okay?"

"Sure. It seems like I've waited for ages to hear this."

"Good. It began when I was almost five. As you have seen, I had no neighbors nearby to play with, but one day, a boy my age showed up in my bedroom, which was also my playroom. I assumed my mother escorted him in, and we played with my toys for a while. He said his name was Jason. At lunchtime, I asked Mom if Jason was staying for lunch with us. She did not know anything about him, and when we looked around, we could not find him in the room. I played with him again after lunch, then at mid-afternoon, Mom came up to my room to see if I was going to take a nap. I mentioned playing with Jason again. She scooped me up and chucked me on the bed and told me she did not want to hear any more talk about this Jason kid who I could see but she obviously could not see.

"That took place in the late winter. Jason would come back to play with me in my room, and also outside in the yard and barn when the weather warmed up. On into the summer, Jason asked if he could bring along some friends to play with us, and of course, I said yes. He soon brought along three friends whose names were Tommy, Nancy, and Crystal." Crystal gasped at the mention of her name and then smiled. "The five of us had a great time playing outside most of the time, as the weather was usually nice. They did not visit nearly as often through the colder months, but sometimes I could play outside in the winter as well.

"When the weather warmed up again, and I was outside most of the time, my friends returned more regularly. One day that fall, Jason called me aside and asked me to take a walk with him down the laneway towards the back of the property. On our walk, he told me that pretty soon he would no longer be able to come and play with me as he had something else he needed to do. I cried. He was the best friend I had ever had. A month later, Mom delivered a baby boy. She named him Jason. As soon as Jason and I looked into each other's eyes, I was sure my two Jason's were one, and I soon felt that even as a baby he remembered playing with me and us having our close friendship.

"Tommy, Nancy, and Crystal continued to come and play with me, just like Jason had promised they would. Before the winter arrived, Crystal took me for a walk down the laneway and pulled a Jason, telling me that soon she would not be able to come and play any longer. I shocked her when I asked if she was going to go into a baby like Jason did. She asked me how I knew that, and I explained that when Jason and I looked into each other's eyes, I knew in my heart that my two Jasons were one. I will never forget your response. You said, *your heart knows,*" I managed to squeak out with a cracking voice and tears trickling down my cheeks.

Crystal scooted over close to me and hugged me tightly. I could also hear her sniffling along with me. We rocked each other lovingly until we got over this sentimental session. Eventually, she released me and wiped the remaining tears from her cheeks with her fingers as she had no supply of tissues. "When you are ready, please go on with your story."

"You also explained to me that you and the other playmates did not have bodies like I did, and that is why my parents could not see any of you, only I could. You added that when I was old enough to understand, then this would be explained to me. Oops, I nearly forgot to say that I was upset when you told me you were going to disappear because after Jason was gone, you became my favorite playmate." Crystal reached over and kissed my cheek.

"For two years, Nancy and Tommy continued to come and play with me. Then one day, with Tommy present, Nancy advised me that she would also soon stop coming to visit me. It did not surprise me that much this time around because Mom had recently explained to Jason and me that we would soon have a baby brother or sister. I asked Nancy if she was going to be my new sister, and she said yes. I asked if she would be called Nancy and she explained that Mom would decide on the name, but added that Nancy was the name currently on the top of her list of names for girls. I asked how she knew that, and she said that they could pop in and out anywhere inside the house, just like they did to play with me, but no one could see them, not even me unless they wanted people to see them. Mom had a baby girl and, as you know, she called her Nancy. So, I knew where my playmates Jason and Nancy disappeared to, but I never knew where you disappeared to, but more about that later.

"I asked Tommy if he would someday disappear on me also and he said no, that he would continue to visit with me as he would be my guide. I was eight then and did not know exactly what that meant, but Tommy did not explain it much for many years to come. The years flew by. I went to elementary school in Mantle, but they had no high school, so I was off to Promenade for four years. I started college in Cincinnati, but first year did not last long. My college roommate had a car. Five weeks into my first year we were out on Saturday evening cruising for chicks when I momentarily heard tires squeal and my lights went out." Crystal gave me a curious look.

"I'll explain. The driver of another car, also one of our own students, missed a stop sign and crashed into me and the passenger door. This is the honest to God truth. The next thing I remember, I was sitting in a really nice place, having a conversation with my deceased grandfather about our fishing adventures together. It was beautiful there. There were others around, but I don't recall recognizing any of the others, just Grandpa. After a while, he looked up and said I had to go back. Then poof, everything went blank again. I have no idea how long that lasted of course, but then suddenly I was back talking with my Grandpa. That visit did not last as long as the first, and soon, everything went blank again.

"I eventually woke up very groggy, in a hospital room with a congregation of relatives and medical staff huddled around me. I suffered head and internal injuries, a shattered right thigh bone and a broken right arm. Mom told me much later that my heart had stopped twice in the operating room, so that apparently explained my two visits with Grandpa in Heaven. It really was a nice place. I was in the hospital for over seven months, including rehab time, before I was allowed to go home for the summer. In September, I started my first year of college all over again.

"Tommy and I agreed when I was about thirteen that it was time for us to become Tom and John instead of Tommy and Johnny. Tom visited with me at times while I was in the hospital, but he needed to carefully pick his visits. He could pop out in an instant at any time, so that was not the problem. He was worried if a doctor or nurse walked in unexpectedly, and he disappeared, it would appear to the visitor that I was talking away to nobody. They might just wonder if my head injuries were worse than they had suspected.

"Tom was my regular companion when I was home for the summer. When they allowed me to leave the hospital for the summer, they insisted I continue my rehab, which included a lot of walking. That is when my off and on morning and evening walks became etched in stone. Whenever I had asked Tom in the past how all of this popping in and out of rooms and bodies worked, he always told me I was not ready to hear the answers.

"After I experienced my visits with Grandpa in what I presumed was Heaven, it was difficult for Tom to keep giving me the excuse that I wasn't ready. He confirmed that my soul did, indeed, leave my body and travel to Heaven when my body was temporarily dead. He also confirmed that he was my Spirit Guide for this lifetime and would not incarnate in a body in this cycle, as this time around his responsibility was to be my Spirit Guide. I asked him if he knew where you were, and he said yes, and he added that he looked in on you often. He explained that all of my invisible friends, as well as my parents, your parents, me and also many other souls, were all part of the same soul group and we reincarnated a number of times together, but not usually in the same relationship. For example, you could have been my daughter in one past life and my father in a different one. He said souls are sexless, and it is the bodies that we reside in that are male and female.

"I asked where you were, and he said he could not tell me because your information was confidential to you and not for everyone to know about. He did say because we were both in the same soul group, then it was possible our paths might someday cross, but that depended on our free will decisions because our decisions determine our future. He used my accident to explain free will. If I had gone to college in Chicago, then I would never have been in the accident in Cincinnati. I asked if I would have been in an accident in Chicago instead, and he answered that we will never know because I was not in Chicago. Well, I guess that is a very long explanation of why I was so happy when you thought you recognized our barn even though you had never been here before. Your conscious mind did not recognize the barn, but your soul did because you visited and played in it numerous times before you incarnated in your body. Make sense?"

Crystal flashed that marvelous grin of hers and gingerly maneuvered around so she could fling her left leg over my legs to straddle me. She shuffled forward a bit so she could wrap her arms around my neck and then initiated another one of our explosive kissing sessions. Faithful to her promise to my mother, nothing inappropriate materialized.

8

On Sunday afternoon when my parents were busy with their own activities, Crystal took my hand in hers and quietly said, "Let's go outside for a while," so away we went. I assumed we were off for another walk to the rear of the farm, but she fooled me when she led me directly to the barn and up the ladder to the hayloft. We left the comforter and straw bales in place the day before after I shared my secrets concerning my visits with my invisible friends and my Grandpa when I was on the operating table after my automobile accident. She sat down and leaned against my straw bale. "Come. Sit down close to me so we can cuddle while we talk."

Of course, I willingly complied, and we immediately enjoyed another series of passionate embraces that left us both panting and dealing with elevated hormone levels. Crystal pulled her head away from me and whispered, "Okay, tiger, enough smooching for now. We need to allow ourselves time to cool down. We can snuggle, but that's it." We cuddled silently for maybe ten minutes without a word between us, and then Crystal interrupted our silence.

"I was sincerely thrilled to hear your story of your experiences with your invisible friends and even more so with your visits to your grandfather in Heaven. That one was a real shocker. I want to now share with you the story of my visits with my invisible friends, and there is certainly a lot of similarity in our two experiences.

"I think I was also around five when Courtney began to visit me outside when I was playing by myself. We did not live on a farm like this, but it was a house in the country very similar to your surrounding area here, except that the crops were different. Have you ever heard of Horseshoe Bend Township in Kentucky?"

"Not that I recall."

"I'm not surprised. It is not very big and is sparsely populated. It got its name from a river which is now only a small stream. If you look at the township on a map, you can see that the stream actually looks like an enormous horseshoe. Going back hundreds of years, or maybe even longer, the entire township on the inside of the horseshoe was apparently a small lake with the river running in and out of it on the north side of the lake. This lake is the reason our township is blessed with a unique type of sandy loam, which is excellent for growing vegetables of all kinds.

"I know it sounds like I am digressing a bit from the story of my invisible friends, but I'm actually not really doing that. Besides, I love to share with others the history of our incredible past. When the waves and waves of immigrants were arriving in our country and were migrating west, a few of them discovered the unique soils in our area. Some of the experienced farmers from the old country decided to reside there instead of continuing further west. They somehow obtained a grant for the land inside the horseshoe and agreed amongst themselves to divide up this fertile land and help each other build homes as well as begin farming. I have no idea where they obtained the seeds to plant there but can only assume they brought some from the old country. They were all pretty successful. They began selling their vegetables and fruits to passing settlers as well as residents in surrounding communities that were springing up.

"My great-great-grandfather was not one of the original settlers there, but a later settler passing through. He had a farming background back in England, recognized the unique growing qualities of the land in the horseshoe and decided that he wanted to stay there. One of the most successful growers needed farm help, and he hired my great-great-grandfather to work for him. He lived with his employer at first, and faithfully saved his earnings for the future. One day, a few years later, when another group of settlers travelling west passed through, he met a young lady that he instantly became infatuated with. I guess the feeling was mutual because, after only a few days, he asked her father for her hand in marriage. Her father agreed. Her father assumed my great-great-grandfather would join them on their journey west, and my great-great-grandfather advised his employer he was leaving.

"His employer did not want to lose his friend and faithful worker, so he needed to figure out how to keep my great-great-grandfather there on his farm. He told my great-great-grandfather that if he would remain there on the farm and continue working for him, he would give my great-great-grandfather a piece of land and help him build a new home for himself and his bride. The girl's father was not pleased with this wrinkle in his own plans, but his daughter apparently took the side of her betrothed. The story goes that she pointed out to her father that she would have a husband who adored her and wanted to marry her, and also a new house to live in, and asked what more could a father want for a daughter than that. She won her argument. A preacher in a nearby village married them immediately, and her parents continued on their journey west.

"My great-great-grandfather was fifteen years older than his bride who was twenty, I believe. No one seems to be able to explain the reason, but it was over twenty years before she delivered her one and only child, my great-grandfather. My great-great-grandfather was fifty-five at the time of the birth. Father and son had a wonderful relationship, according to my grandfather, but the huge age difference prevented them from enjoying a lot of the usual father and son activities. Fishing, a less energetic activity, was their favorite sport. My great-great-grandfather died when my great-grandfather was twenty. He inherited the house along with his mother, who lived another twenty years.

"My great-grandparents had two daughters first and then a son, my grandfather. The girls married locally, and my grandfather inherited the house when his father died. I should add that all of my male ancestors continued to work on the farm for the family of the original settler who built the house, so my great-great-grandfather did not leave to go west. My grandfather passed along a few years ago and my dad, the only son out of four children, inherited the family house. Mom and Dad still live in this original house in the country. It has been remodeled along the way, and an addition was put on when my grandparents had four children. My dad was the first of the male descendants to not continue the tradition of working on the farm for the original family. That is where I grew up and where Courtney came to visit me."

"That is an interesting story of how two families continued to be closely associated for generations," I commented.

"It certainly is. The families are still close. Courtney was my best friend after she arrived. There were a few other children in our rural area, but no girls close to my age. My mother could watch me through various windows in the house as I ran around and played outside. One day when I came in for lunch, she asked me who I was playing without there when I was making so much noise. I said Courtney. She asked me where Courtney lived. I told her I did not know and that she just showed up in the yard to play with me many days. Mom just grinned and left it at that. A number of years later Mom shared with me the fact that she also played with invisible friends when she was growing up, so she was not the least bit surprised when I appeared to have invisible playmates as well. I was happy to know that I wasn't some weirdo with friends only I could see.

"I think it was the year after Courtney began playing with me that she asked if she could bring along a couple of other girls to play with us. I said sure, and a few days later June and Juliet arrived with Courtney. They appeared to be about our age. The four of us had a wonderful time playing lots of games. After I started school that year, I had less time to play and therefore received less visits from the girls.

"One weekend, not too long before Christmas, we were playing outside on a nice day for December, when Courtney called all of us together for a pow-wow but she was really talking to me. She said that in a few weeks June and Juliet would likely no longer be able to return and play with us anymore. I was quite saddened by the terrible news and asked why. Courtney replied that there was someplace else they needed to go to, but she was not able to provide any of the details to me. Sound familiar? She also assured me that she was never going to disappear on me like the other girls would likely do. A month later, my mother gave birth to twin girls. She called them June and Juliet. As you know, at home we called them Junie and Julie. Like you, when I looked into their eyes, I knew they were really my playmates June and Juliet.

"The years passed by and Courtney was my primary playmate and best friend. She still is my best friend. Well, until you came along. She's number two now," Crystal said with a wide grin.

I grabbed her and immediately initiated the first of a wild series of embraces that soon left us lying on the comforter panting and gasping for air. This woman is a miracle sent to me from Heaven, I thought to myself.

Okay, this is me now, the old geezer. Think about it. What are the statistical odds that by pure chance the woman that I knew about twenty-five years earlier, as a spirit playmate for only a few months, would walk back into my life from a couple hundred miles away by applying for a job at the school I was teaching at, and even in the same department I was teaching in? Then, she has difficulty locating a place to live in a new town when she has no driver's license or car to drive, so our principal phones me to see if I knew of any places where she could rent an apartment or room out in my direction so I could become her chauffeur to and from school. Without even knowing her name yet, I probably had some influence in getting my mother to offer her my sister's old room, and this actually made it all fall into place, but the odds against the entire scenario must be pretty high. A million to one comes to mind, but I have absolutely no idea how accurate that might be. Let me conclude this diversion and say I personally have no doubts whatsoever that it was all meant to be, or prearranged by our souls in the spirit world, or Heaven, or whatever term you wish to use. Okay, back to Crystal's story.

"I made friends at my rural elementary school, and later on in the secondary school, they bussed us to, like they did for you, in a larger town further away. I would classify them as friends, not good friends. Courtney had no competition for the best friend position. Even in college, my friends were passing and no competition for Courtney. Sound's a lot like you and Tom doesn't it?"

I grinned. "You've got that right."

"I thought so. Okay, I am almost finished. Like you, as I got older, I asked Courtney more and more questions about how all of this popping in and out by spirits worked. Like Tom, she answered some of my questions and also gave me the *later* answer that you heard so often from Tom. I did have one advantage that you apparently did not have once Mom admitted to me when I was about sixteen that she also experienced spirit visits or invisible playmates. Mom said that Dad did not believe any of this stuff, so Mom needed to pick her opportunities carefully for us to talk about our invisible friends. Similar to you and Tom, Courtney first mentioned that she would stick around throughout my life and act as my guide, and later on, used the term Spirit Guide. She also explained about our soul group and used our family as the example but did not mention you as you were not part of my human life at that time.

"When I shared the conversations between Courtney and me with Mom, she told me her Spirit Guide was called Mayra. Mayra had explained the happenings that we both experienced pretty much like Courtney explained them to me. Of course, that made me quite excited, as it was a wonderful verification that I was not just some hallucinating young girl with a warped imagination. What a relief."

I figured Crystal was finished with her story, so I grabbed her once again, initiating another round of explosive embraces that left the two of us delightfully exhausted and flaked out on our backs on the comforter. I am definitely addicted to this, I thought to myself.

Eight or ten minutes later, still flashing a cheek-to-cheek

grin, Crystal propped her head upon her left hand. "Going back to our invisible friends, correct me if I am wrong, you said that Tom told you that he, my family, and your family were all part of the same soul group. Courtney told me that she and my family were all part of the same soul group, right?"

"Right."

"That means Tom and Courtney are also in the same soul group, right?"

"That should be correct."

"Tom would not tell you anything significant about me because you did not know the human me, right?"

"Right."

"Now that we both know each other, there should be no reason why you and I, along with Tom and Courtney, cannot all be together having one conversation, is there?"

"It makes sense to me."

"Good. Why don't you take a walk out your laneway for a few minutes and along your way ask Tom to visit with you. If he shows up, ask if there is any reason why the four of us cannot get together and chat. While you are gone, I will try and contact Courtney and ask her the same question, okay?"

Headed towards the back of the farm, I waited only about two minutes. "Tom, if you are here with me, please appear." He immediately popped in beside me. "That was quick. Did you hear the conversation between Crystal and me in the hayloft a few minutes ago?"

"I did."

"Good. So, is it possible for you and me along with Crystal and Courtney to assemble together for a group conversation? We all know about each other and are in the same soul group, right?"

"That is correct and yes we can."

"Fantastic." I walked casually back towards the barn not

47

wishing to arrive before Crystal finished her conversation with Courtney, assuming Courtney was also hanging around. I quietly walked into the barn before stopping and listening for voices in the hayloft. I heard none. "How did it go up there?" I called out.

"We are just sitting around waiting for you guys to show up." I giggled and climbed up the ladder to the loft. Tom popped in next to me. "John, I would like you to finally meet my Spirit Guide, Courtney."

"Hi, Courtney, nice to meet you," I called out to the young woman who appeared to be approximately the same age as Crystal. I am not sure if I ever mentioned it before, but as I aged, so did Tom. It made sense when I thought about it that as us children grew older; we would likely feel more comfortable around a guide that was our own age instead of one who remained a young child.

"It is nice to meet you finally as well, John."

"Crystal, say hello to Tom."

"Hi, Tom. I am honored to finally meet you. I have certainly heard a lot about you."

"I know. He talks a lot. I am thrilled to finally meet you as well, Crystal."

"I gather that you and Courtney already know each other?" I said, turning to Tom.

"Only for many thousands of years through numerous incarnation cycles."

"We go back that far?" Crystal asked with a shocked look on her face.

"That we do," Tom replied. "Was there a specific reason you two wanted the four of us to get together?"

I caught Crystal's eye and nodded. She understood. "Well, first off, I wanted to meet you, Tom, and, of course, I wanted John to meet Courtney. Secondly, I wanted to see if we understood correctly exactly what questions you and Courtney would answer, now that John and I have re-found each other. Thirdly, you told John many years ago that his family and my family, as well as you, were all in the same soul group. My mother told me years back that she also had invisible friends and a Spirit Guide named Mayra. Do you also know Mayra then?"

"Of course. She is part of our soul group also," Tom answered.

"Good. So, if the four of us got together with my mother and Mayra, could we have a group discussion with the six of us?"

"As long as your mother and John agreed to that. Mayra would have no problem with it as long as your mother and John were in favor of it."

"Okay, taking this a step further. You, John, Nancy, Justin, and I all played together here in this barn when John was five and a bit older. Could we also add Justin and Nancy to a group discussion as well?"

"We could, after you all met each other and also agreed to do so. You have never met the human Justin or Nancy. Then you would need to share with the others at least some of your experiences with your invisible friends and vice versa, just like you and John did yesterday and today. Do you understand?"

"I think so. So, the same would apply with my mother and John?"

"That would be best, but because the three of you already know each other and have all had similar experiences with spirit visitors, then you all possess a similar understanding of what is going on with us pop-in artists."

Crystal giggled. "That makes sense. I guess that is all I need to ask for now. I gather we can hold these groups-of-four get-togethers any time then?"

"Anytime. Courtney and I are always hanging around you

and John. Is there anything else you would like to add, Court-ney? I have been doing all of the answering."

"You did an excellent job," Courtney replied and then disappeared, immediately followed by Tom.

"This is making more and more sense all the time," Crystal said to me.

9

The weeks sailed by. Schoolwork kept us busy. Crystal and I still continued our evening walks, unless the weather was too bad, and also snatched every morning opportunity to walk when we could. Our hayloft hideaway became our private love-making hangout. We experimented with numerous pleasurable activities that did not result in depriving my loved one of her virginity.

Once Crystal and I became girlfriend and boyfriend, which we continued to keep a secret from everyone except our two families, Mom and Crystal's mother began to telephone each other on a regular basis, becoming good, long-distance friends. We had not visited Crystal's parents throughout the school year to that point in time, so Cassandra insisted we do so for the special holidays like Thanksgiving and Christmas. Mom and Cassandra worked out our schedules over the telephone lines. Mom held our Thanksgiving get-together on Thursday so we could travel to Horseshoe Bend Township on Friday for the Wilson family get-together on Saturday, allowing us to drive back to my place on Sunday for school on Monday.

Of course, Nancy did not make it from Paris for Thanksgiving, but Jason, fortunately, had the Thursday off, so he drove home on Thursday morning to spend the day with us. It was great to see him again, even if it was a rather short visit. Jason shared with the family for the first time that he began dating a female, fellow Kentucky State Police officer and would have brought her with him but she was working until Saturday at three in the afternoon and would drive home after that to spend part of the Holiday weekend with her family.

Both Junie and Julie were home when we arrived in Horseshoe Bend Township. Like Crystal, they did not have a driver's license or a vehicle at their disposal, so Martin picked them up Wednesday after classes at Lexington's University of Kentucky and brought them home for the weekend. Junie had a boyfriend who did not join us as he also went home to his family for the weekend. Julie enjoyed lots of dates but preferred to play the field as opposed to settling for one boyfriend. I really enjoyed the twins. They were fraternal twins, not identical twins. Looking at them, no one would even suspect they were twins. Julie was blonde like Crystal and Cassandra and looked a lot like Crystal. Julie and Crystal were not just lookalikes but pretty much had similar personalities, being rather quiet and reserved. Junie was a redhead like her father and a bubbling bundle of chatter that no one in any room full of people could miss. She was also an accomplished flirt which I could tell irritated Crystal when I, the only bachelor in the house, became the center of her attention much of the time.

The Wilson family home had been originally a three-bedroom house before the addition was built when the twins were preteens, so they shared a bedroom until then, but after the fourth bedroom and family room were added, the twins enjoyed their own privacy. Crystal told me on our drive back to my place that when I was busy chatting with Martin on Friday after our arrival, Cassandra waved her into the kitchen and asked if she and I were sharing a bedroom. She truthfully said that we were not. Crystal told Cassandra that she would give me her bedroom and bunk in with Julie while we were there. That solved a problem that Cassandra had apparently been stewing over since we agreed to spend some of the holiday with them. Before I move on with my story, I want to share with you the fact that Crystal was part of an absolutely fantastic family, and I have enjoyed them for a lifetime.

After a marvelous weekend with our two families, I was sure I added five pounds to my waistline, but we faithfully got back into our walking routines once we returned home. As the Christmas break approached, I gave serious consideration to presenting Crystal with a marriage proposal. I was sure she would say yes, but in the end, I decided it would be wise to allow her more time to get to know me even better, so I bought her an amazing gold necklace with a shiny birthstone on it for her Christmas present. Because we had a two-week Christmas break, we were able to spend a week with each family.

Winters were not too bad in general where we lived, and that winter we did not receive much snow at all. The school year continued to zip along, and Easter loomed rapidly ahead of us. One day when Crystal was holed up in her bedroom marking essays, I asked Mom if she still possessed her mother's engagement ring.

"And what might you want to know that for, young man?" she replied with a smile that would melt an ice cube, even though she knew perfectly well what I had in mind.

"I want to sell it, so I have enough money to fly alone to Mexico for a couple weeks this summer," I teased her back.

She took her right hand and slowly pretended she was going to smack me across the side of my head but allowed me plenty of time to duck. Mom and I quietly went upstairs to my parent's room, and she retrieved the ring from her jewelry box. It was beautiful, as I remembered it, even though I had not seen it for a number of years. There was a larger but not huge diamond in the center of two smaller ones. Mom kept it in a small plastic bag with air holes in it, I assumed to prevent it from tarnishing, but I knew absolutely nothing about jewelry. I tucked it carefully in the bottom of a front pocket in my jeans. "Thank you. Is it alright if I present it to our favorite young lady?"

"I wouldn't have it any other way."

Crystal and I took our usual evening walk after dinner. Spring had arrived, and the weather was awesome. At the conclusion of our walk, we took our now habitual detour up to the hayloft for another hot and heavy addition of our non-copulation lovemaking. After an extended cooling-out period, I moved close to Crystal and propped myself up on my right hand. "I have a question for you," I said in a loud whisper.

"I'm listening," she whispered back, propping herself up on her left hand.

"Will you marry me?"

Crystal's face lit up like a grinning Christmas tree. "Well, I have a question for you too."

Oh, oh, I thought. This is not good. "Okay, I'm listening."

"What took you so long?" she teased and barreled me over before initiating another round of heavy petting. We revved our engines up so high we could have lit the straw beneath us on fire if Mom's old comforter was not acting as insulation. My manhood was trying to burst through the leg of my jeans and Crystal must have noticed it, as she often did, but for the very first time she placed her hand on it and began to gently caress it. I wiggled around in desperation; afraid I would explode.

She removed her hand from my shotgun and lay on her

back. "We can celebrate our engagement by going all the way," she cooed.

I sat up and stared at her beautiful, smiling face. My manhood screamed yes, but my soul said no. "Thank you for that precious gift, but I am going to take a raincheck on your offer. You told me many months ago that you always wanted to be a virgin on your wedding night, and you really are going to be a virgin on our wedding night."

Crystal looked shocked at first, but then her marvelous smile returned. "I hope you know how much I love you," she whispered.

"I am sure I have a pretty good idea because I love you even more." I stood up and removed Grandma's engagement ring from my jean's pocket before plopping down on both knees next to her. "Your left hand, please." Crystal sat up and extended her hand to me so I could slip the ring on her finger. "This was my mom's mother's engagement ring. Mom has been saving it for years for the right occasion to present itself. I asked her for it earlier today, and she was delighted to know who would be the next lady to wear it. If you prefer, we can go to the jewelry store in town, and you can pick a different one out yourself."

Crystal studied the ring for a few seconds. "Nope! This ring was destined for me."

10

On our way back to the house to share our fantastic news with my parents, I mentioned that it made more sense to me that we schedule our wedding during summer vacation instead of sometime during the school year. "Do you prefer this summer, or would you rather wait until next summer?"

"Do you want to wait another year before we enjoy all of the pleasures of married life?"

"Not really, I must admit."

"Good, I second that motion. I only want a small wedding with close family members so it will not be too difficult to organize that for this summer. All of my Kentucky ancestors have been married in our little nondenominational church in Horseshoe Bend Township, and I hope you will agree to my wish to continue that family tradition."

"I do not care where we get married. All I care about is that we do get married."

"Good, that's settled."

After we were inside the house Crystal took off like a tornado screeching, "We're engaged, we're engaged," at the top of her lungs. Mom and Dad were in the living room, and when she heard the squeals from my excited betrothed, Mom met her flying, future daughter-in-law before she landed. The two girls hugged each other warmly, and happy tears flowed freely down many cheeks, including mine. I knew these two adored each other, but it was heartwarming to witness this open display of happiness their celebration conveyed.

Dad detoured around the blubbering couple and joined me at my observation post. "Congratulations, son," he said, extending his hand. "You are an extremely fortunate fellow to have caught a prized gal like Crystal."

"Believe me, Dad, I know it."

Because still no one at school or in town even knew Crystal and I were dating, we agreed that she would only wear her engagement ring when with our families. I often worried that she might forget to take it off in the morning if we were running late on our usual departure time for our drive to school, but it never happened that I am aware of. I am pretty sure that if she was wearing the ring at school, someone would have noticed it, so I am almost positive she never forgot to take it off on those mornings.

We were married in the middle of July in the quaint little white church that was only a walking distance from Crystal's family's home. It was definitely a small wedding. Her parents and the twins were present on her side and my parents, Jason and his co-worker, police officer, now girlfriend Bridget, represented my side of the family. I know it all sounds pretty sparse to many readers, but that was exactly the way Crystal wanted it. Martin treated all of us to a lovely dinner in a private room in the classiest restaurant in their nearby town, and that was our wedding reception.

We did not go on our honeymoon immediately, but we did sleep in the same bed for the first time on our wedding night in Crystal's bedroom at the Wilson home. We behaved ourselves. Crystal began using the birth control pills as soon as we were engaged, so that was not the reason she remained a virgin on her wedding night. With four occupied bedrooms upstairs, we were sure not going to make a lot of racket on our wedding night. That was actually okay with us as before the wedding we agreed that the appropriate location for Crystal to sacrifice her virginity was where she first offered it to me when I respectfully declined - our hayloft hideaway. We drove home from Horseshoe Bend Township the next day, and after our evening walk, we christened our wonderful marriage for the first time up in our hayloft hideaway. Crystal was self-conscious about having sex in my bedroom, which became our bedroom, because of the proximity of my parent's bedroom, so for the time being, all of our pleasurable connections were enjoyed in the hayloft where we could make all of the noise we desired.

Prior to the wedding, the four of us sat down and discussed housing options. With Jason living hours away and the free-spirited Nancy showing no signs of leaving Paris, Dad figured I would inherit the family home. He also brought up the reality that I effectively owned over half of it anyway after paying off their mortgage with my accident settlement. Dad offered to move Mom and him into town and leave us the privacy of the big old house, but Crystal quickly nixed that idea. She insisted that the four of us got along so well that there was no need to break up the family just because of a wedding ceremony. She also added that when we eventually had a few children, it would be very nice to have Grandma around as babysitter when she returned to her teaching position. Everyone agreed that Crystal's take on the situation was the best option, at least for the present.

In August Crystal and I flew from Cincinnati to Los Angeles for our honeymoon. She always wanted to experience a close-up view of the movie stars of Hollywood, and we enjoyed a marvelous time before we needed to get ready for the new school year. I never mentioned it earlier, I don't think, but at the final staff meeting in June, I announced to the staff that Crystal and I had been secretly dating for some time now and we were going to be married at a small family gathering in July. We received lots of congratulations, but I assume some of the staff suspected that Crystal had become pregnant along the way and therefore we were doing everything quick and low-key. As you know, that was not the case at all, and the staff would eventually get the proof when no baby bump appeared. She happily took our family name, so when school started, Miss Wilson became Mrs. Tranter.

11

Three years seemed to zoom by rather quickly. They were wonderful years but basically uneventful until the spring of the third year. The English Department Head, my former senior English teacher, decided to retire at the end of the year. I applied for and was awarded the position of Head of the English Department. Next, we needed to deal with the filling of the vacant position. The Principal, the retiring head, and I formed a committee of three, in case the decision came to a vote, and we advertised the vacancy. The remaining teachers in the English Department were Crystal and I, along with two middle-aged ladies. Our committee hoped we could add another male to the department, but quality remained the primary criteria. That was still back in the era of teacher shortages, so we received three applications for the vacant position, two men and one lady. We invited the two men in first for interviews, and we considered them okay at best.

That left Abigail Slaughter. She possessed an impressive resume, and we hoped for the best. If I have only one word to describe her, it would certainly be unique. She was a bubbly redhead that instantly reminded me of Crystal's sister, Junie, except for her appearance. Abigail was five foot ten, without heels, which she did not wear to the interview. She had square shoulders like a football player yet was blessed with an attractive female figure. She was an all-star basketball player in high school, received a full-ride college basketball scholarship, and was a college all-star as well. She shared with us the fact that her father had been a college football lineman. She definitely inherited many of his physical attributes. Her English teaching qualifications were quite good, and she won us all over when she revealed that she would love to coach our girls' basketball team if the position ever became open. Our current basketball coach only had experience playing high school basketball, and originally needed to be arm-twisted to coach our girls' team. Abigail also mentioned that everyone called her Abie. We signed her up immediately.

Abie was introduced to the staff at the end-of-year staff meeting, but she previously met a few of the staff on the day we signed her up when I took her on a guided tour of our building. She, of course, met Crystal who was still in the building waiting for her ride home. The two ladies hit it off immediately, as they were fairly close to the same age and now part the same department. When she signed her contract, the principal gave Abie a staff list which included home telephone numbers.

Crystal and I discovered later that Abie first looked around for an apartment to rent, but there was nothing that caught her attention. Shortly thereafter she returned to Promenade with her father and they went house hunting. They were country folk like Crystal and I, so when they heard about the estate sale of an older house on a large country lot between Promenade and Mantle, they checked it out. It needed a good cleaning and some minor repairs, but its structure was built to last forever. It also came with all of the furniture of the recently deceased gentleman, some of which were now antiques and some of which was now junk. Abie and her father worked on the house for a month and made it not just livable but comfortably livable. She moved in at the beginning of August. She had phoned Crystal and me twice through July to say hello and advise us on how the renovations were progressing, but she did not invite us over to see it at that juncture.

In early August, Mom answered the telephone as we were enjoying our morning coffee after breakfast. "It's Abie. She asked for one of you guys."

Crystal nodded at me to take the call. "Good morning, Abie. How's it going?"

"Well. I have an interesting problem. I think my lovely country home is haunted."

"Oh my. What happened?"

"I was awake in the middle of the night and decided to go downstairs and get a drink of milk. That was actually the first time that I ever ventured downstairs during any of the nights that I've slept here. While I was in the kitchen, I heard this female voice in the basement screaming, 'Noooooooooo, noooooooooo, nooooooooo.' I know there was nobody down there and I hustled back upstairs as fast as I could. I could not hear the piercing voice from upstairs. In the morning, I ate breakfast at the kitchen table as I usually do, and all was quiet. After I finished eating, I was brave enough, accompanied by my longest butcher knife, to slowly sneak down the basement stairs. Nobody was there, and nothing appeared to have been knocked over or moved around. The only thing I can think of is that I have inherited an unhappy ghost with my house purchase. Do you know of anyone in our vicinity who can cleanse houses of earthbound spirits?"

I needed a little time to mull that over for a minute.

"John, are you still there?"

"Sorry, Abie. I was thinking here for a minute. Are you going to be home after lunch?"

"Yes."

"Good. Let me work on your little problem for a while, then Crystal and I will drive over and see you after lunch, okay?"

"Wonderful."

Abie gave me the directions to her new residence. It was not directly on our driving route to school, but I had driven past her house numerous times in my lifetime, so I knew approximately where it was situated and would have no problem finding it.

"What is going on?" Crystal asked as I returned to my cooling coffee.

I sighed. "She thinks her house may be haunted because she heard a female voice screaming in the basement when she went down to the kitchen for a drink in the middle of the night."

"Why is she calling you?" Mom asked.

"She really doesn't know very many people around here yet, and I guess she had to ask someone for advice."

"What does she expect you to do?" Mom continued.

"She is hoping that she can locate someone who is experienced at cleansing houses of unwanted spirits. I needed a little time to see if I could think of ever hearing of anyone who might be able to do this. When we visit her, she may share more details about her experience, and maybe I will come up with some ideas in the meantime."

"I see," Mom said, apparently satisfied.

I had a plan in mind, but it was not something I could share with a mother who told me at age four or five she did not want to hear any more about my invisible friend. When we finished our coffees, I asked Crystal to join me outside for another walk, and of course, she did. "I want to call in Tom and Courtney for a group pow-wow," I explained to my sweetheart when we were out of hearing range. "Tom, if you and Courtney are around, please appear." Tom popped in beside me immediately.

"Crystal needs to invite Courtney, not you," Tom advised.

"Courtney, if you are here, please show yourself," Crystal said, and her Spirit Guide materialized beside her.

"Did you two hear our conversation in the kitchen a few minutes ago?" I asked.

"I didn't," Tom said. "We come pretty much immediately when called, but we are not snooping around at what you are doing twenty-four-seven."

That's probably a good thing, I thought to myself, as there were times Crystal and I were enjoying married life where we did not need an audience, human or ghostly. "I understand." I explained Abie's telephone call to Tom and Courtney. "Is it possible for you two to tag along with Crystal and me when we visit Abie's basement and see if you can make contact with the spirit that is apparently stuck down there, or at least visiting there at times?"

"This isn't part of our job description," Tom quipped.

Crystal and I roared with laughter.

"I am just teasing you," Tom continued. "We will be happy to tag along with you this afternoon when you visit with Abie. Ask her early to take you down to the basement so you can look around, and after that, if you can swing it see if you can get her to sit outside, if she has any lawn chairs, or take a stroll around her property. Courtney and I will remain in the basement and see if we can make contact with the spirit lady. It is best if we can get Abie out of hearing range."

"Excellent. Do you think you can get the spirit to cross over?" I asked.

"Maybe. We will have a better idea when we know why the spirit got stuck there in the first place and did not cross over at the original time of death. There is also a possibility that some humorous but nasty spirit is playing games with Abie for entertainment."

"Is that common?"

"No, but there is a slim chance."

"Anything else you want us to do?"

"Not at this point. We will see how this afternoon goes and go from there."

We pulled into Abie's driveway a little after one-thirty. She was lounging in a lawn chair in front of her house. "Thank you so much for coming," she said and gave us both a quick hug. "This is going to quickly drive me absolutely bonkers if I don't get it resolved pronto. Have you got any good news for me?"

"Unfortunately, no, but I assure you that we are still working on it. Could you please take us down to the basement first thing?"

"Of course. Follow me."

Abie led us along the hallway to the kitchen and over to the closed and locked door to the cellar. In these older houses, like ours as well, cellars were rarely finished like they often are in modern times, and they were usually pretty dingy-looking spaces. Most included a fruit cellar for storing home-made preserves and the rest of the space often inherited odds and ends that were no longer being used but that the owners were not ready to throw out yet. Most of them included a lock on the door so that children could not open it and possibly tumble down the open staircase.

Abie signaled to me that I had the honor of being the brave one in the group to be the first to venture down into the world of the unknown, so I led the parade slowly down into the much cooler basement. The sellers, or more likely Abie and her dad, had done a super job in cleaning up the basement and it did not look very dingy at all. It was pretty much empty except that along the wall on the right there were two ladders leaning against the poured-cement wall, and a number of paint cans lined up next to them. I circled around and under the staircase to the front wall, then slowly walked along the circumference of the decent-sized basement looking for anything at all that might be of interest. The girls ventured into the center of the floor under the only light and observed my travels from that vantage point. I did a second go-round, not that I expected to find anything exciting, but to allow Tom and Courtney more time to arrive if they needed it. I then joined the girls under the light. "I do not see anything out of the ordinary."

"I know. I didn't either when I snuck down here this morning, but I swear to you that I heard a screeching female voice in the night," Abie exclaimed. "It wasn't just a scream but an elongated nooooooo, over and over. It was too damn loud to be imaginary."

"Don't worry, I believe you," I replied, giving her shoulder a gentle squeeze for assurance. "Let's go back upstairs."

Abie locked the cellar door again and took us on a guided tour of her new home. I was impressed. She and her father did a marvelous decorating job. At the conclusion of our tour, the staircase from the second floor brought us down into the foyer at the front door.

"Can you spare a little time to sit outside for a while and visit? I have beer, iced tea, and orange juice if you are interested in a drink."

Crystal and I chose the iced tea, and Abie grabbed a beer. I hoped that was not a sign of future problems, but for the present anyway, I chalked it up to her poor night's sleep and unwanted basement squatter. It turned out that my momentary fears were totally unfounded. Like most of us, she enjoyed an occasional beer or two, but she certainly never showed any sign of having a drinking problem.

"Well, have you come up with any possible solutions for my little problem?" she asked when we were settled into our lawn chairs.

"Not really, but I assure you once more that we are definitely working on it. I have some ideas to check into, but it is best that I do not say anything just yet in case I get your hopes up and then disappoint you, okay?" I said.

Abie sighed. "Okay, I understand."

The three of us sipped at our drinks and talked primarily about the fast-approaching new school year for half an hour or so, and then we bid our new colleague goodbye.

12

I had barely driven out of sight of Abie's home when something occurred that had never happened before while driving. Tom and Courtney popped into the rear seat of my new Chevy Impala in unison without being invited. "Pull over, please," Courtney requested. I did so immediately.

"We were in the basement with you three all of the time you were down there," Tom advised us. "It was quite interesting to watch the spirit watch you as you walked around. She would not let you get anywhere near her as you walked. If you came in her direction, she would quickly take off in a different direction. After I picked up on this, I decided to test my theory, so I started walking around like you but nowhere near you, to see if she avoided me also. She did. She had to scamper at times to continue avoiding one or the other of us."

"So, what does that mean?" I asked.

"I am pretty sure she is terrified of men, human or in spirit. So, when you three went back upstairs, I also disappeared, hoping that Courtney could communicate with her in some way while they were alone. Your turn, Courtney."

"When everyone else was gone, I started talking to her

quietly from a distance. I told her that I was there to help her and would not cause her any harm. She seemed to be listening but remained silent. I would take a step or two towards her from time to time as I continued talking. I got to about six feet from her when she stretched her upraised hand out towards me, in what I took as a sign she did not want me to come any closer. I stopped but continued to talk to her. She listened but remained silent. I pointed a finger at me and said, 'Me, Courtney.' She just looked at me. I repeated it a couple more times and then pointed the finger at her saying, 'You.' I thought she replied Katarina, but she has quite an accent and spoke barely above a whisper. I pointed my finger at her again and said, 'You Katarina?' She nodded, yes. I was thrilled with that progress and did not want to push my luck too far on this visit. I asked if it was alright for me to visit her again sometime and she said nothing. I began to wonder if much of her silence was caused by the fact that her English was poor, so I changed my approach. I pointed my finger at me and said, 'Courtney visit Katarina,' pointing the finger from me to her and hoping she understood the word visit. I was thrilled when she again nodded her head, yes. I started stepping backwards away from her and began waving goodbye. I stopped near the staircase and vigorously waved goodbye. She waved back. I blew her a kiss and then popped out. We seemed to have made a connection, and I concluded that it was wise to not push her too far at one time."

"That is wonderful, Courtney," Crystal commented. "You are a miracle worker."

"Oh, I wouldn't say that, but I do have the experience of many lifetimes to draw on as my soul remembers everything that I have experienced in all of those lifetimes. Now we need to talk about our next move. Of course, I want to continue visiting with Katarina, so we can learn more about her and try to help her cross over where she belongs, but I am hesitant to do that behind Abie's back. In fact, I may not even be able to do it behind her back if I wanted to because I am invading her space without her permission. Arriving in the basement with you two and Abie was one thing. On my own is different. Any ideas?"

"You bet," I declared and pulled a quick U-turn after checking for traffic. Abie was reading a book in a lawn chair when we turned back into her driveway. She stood up immediately and walked towards us as Crystal and I got out of my car.

"Did you forget something?"

"No, not that, but we need to have a confidential chat," I replied.

"Okay, come and sit down."

"Actually, it would be better if we went inside, okay?"

"Sure, let's go."

We settled down in the living room on the brand-new sofa set. Abie curiously waited for me to begin the conversation. "First off, what we are going to talk about definitely must remain a secret amongst us. No one at school knows anything about this, okay?"

"I promise it will remain a secret."

"Good. Since you think your basement or home is haunted, then that tells me you pretty much believe that there is survival of spirits after the death of bodies, correct?"

"I guess so."

"When you were young, say age four to six or so, did you ever have or think you had some invisible or imaginary playmates that others could not see?"

"Not that I recall. I was the youngest of five children, so there was no shortage of playmates around."

"Fair enough. Let me tell you about my experiences. It started with one playmate called Jason who my mother could not see and therefore thought I was making it up. Jason and I enjoyed a fantastic time that summer playing outside together in and around the old barn on our farm property. The next spring Jason brought along three other spirit playmates for us. The five of us also had a great time playing together. A year later, one day Jason took me aside and told me that soon he would not be able to return to play with me anymore, but the others would continue to be my playmates. A few weeks after that I had a baby brother. My mother named him Jason."

Abie gasped. "What a coincidence."

"This was no coincidence at all. My spirit friend Jason reincarnated as my brother. I knew it the instant the baby and I looked into each other's eyes, and he apparently knew it also. A little while later this was confirmed by another of my spirit playmates that was named Crystal."

"Oh my God," Abie blurted out.

"I am going to skip some of the details here and just give you the highlights. A few months later, Crystal told me she was going to stop coming to play soon, and before long she disappeared also. I never knew where she went until she applied for the vacant English position at our school four years ago. Two years after Crystal disappeared the other girl in our group, named Nancy, departed to become my new baby sister. Mom called her Nancy."

"This is unreal. Are you making this all up?"

"Not a chance, there is more. With the departure of Jason, then Crystal, and later Nancy, I only had one of my spirit playmates remaining. His name is Tom. Tom assured me that he would not disappear on me like the others because his job was to be my guide throughout this lifetime, and he is still around as my Spirit Guide. He was there with us earlier in your basement as well. Would you like to meet him?"

"Oh my God! You are playing a joke on me, aren't you?"

"This is no joking matter. I do need a yes or a no for him to appear. What do you say?"

"Okay, I'll bite. Yes, I would like to meet him."

"Tom, please present yourself to us." Tom immediately began to slowly materialize near me. Abie watched wide-eyed and speechless. "Tom is a spirit, just like your lady in the basement, but with one big difference. Tom can come and go, or crossover to and from the other side like he did just now. The lady in the basement is apparently an earthbound spirit that did not cross over like most spirits do upon the death of their bodies. She is basically stuck here not knowing what to do to remedy her problem. Tom, say hello to Abie."

"Hello, Abie. I am pleased to meet you. Everything that John told you is the truth, as unrealistic as it may sound at first. When I was in your basement earlier with the three of you, I observed something interesting that I want to share with you. I allowed myself to be seen by your spirit lady, but not the three of you because that would have really freaked you out, I'm sure. As John walked around the basement, the spirit moved away from him whenever he was coming towards her. I then tested my theory by also walking around like John but nowhere near him. The spirit was challenged then to find avenues where she could avoid both of us. A couple of times she walked right by you ladies standing in the middle of the floor and never let that bother her, but she would not let John or I come close to her."

"What does that mean?" Abie asked.

"She is apparently afraid of men but not women."

"Can you get her to leave my basement?"

"I do not think so because of her apparent fear of men, but I know someone who just might be able to accomplish that for you with a bit of work."

"Tell me who."

"It is time for you to hear Crystal's story. Crystal, it's all yours."

"Before coming to Promenade, I never knew John, but I

did have two spirit friends named June and Juliet. They later reincarnated as my twin sisters, June and Juliet. We call then Junie and Julie. Tom was the one who confirmed John's and my belief that I was the reincarnation of John's spirit play-mate, Crystal. I also have a Spirit Guide, but she never was a spirit playmate of mine. Before I continue, let me add that my mother shared with me that she also had spirit playmates as a child. Back to the present, my Spirit Guide's name is Court-ney. She was also with us in the basement earlier. After the three of us went back upstairs and Tom concluded that he should also remove himself from the scene, Courtney was left alone with your spirit lady. Would you like to meet Courtney?"

"Definitely."

"Courtney, please show yourself to us." Courtney slowly materialized beside Crystal.

"Hi, Abie. I really like your house."

Abie smacked her own cheek really hard, and the sound resonated throughout the room, shocking everyone into silence. "I am sorry I startled you. I just wanted to make sure that this is not all a dream. Please share with me how your time with my ghost went."

"She appears quite wary and confused. This is rather common for earthbound spirits, I need to add, as they appar-ently are unable to comprehend what is taking place. I talked to her continually and slowly moved closer and closer towards her until she pushed the palm of her hand towards me. I continued talking quietly to her and realized that she was not saying anything back to me. I pointed a finger at me and said me Courtney. I then pointed a finger at her and said, you. She hesitated but eventually quietly said what I thought was Katarina, with a thick foreign accent. I pointed at her and said Katarina, and she nodded yes. I talked to her some more with no response before I realized she might not know enough English to understand what I was saying at times. I pointed my finger at me and said Courtney visit Katarina, pointing the finger at her then. She nodded her head yes. I was happy that she started to communicate with me and hesitated to push my luck this time around. I slowly walked backwards towards the stairs and began waving goodbye to her. She waved back. I am the main reason why we returned here now. Tom and I came along with John and Crystal this time around, but I will likely continue to come alone in the future. It was imperative that we spring our stories on you before you one day heard the spirit and I having a conversation in your basement. I suspect that would have really freaked you out."

"You bet it would have. I was pretty freaked out earlier just listening to your stories, but thankfully it is now making a lot more sense. I do want to thank all of you for your patience while you enlightened me concerning a world I never even knew existed before. Courtney, are you going to keep me updated after your visits with our spirit friend?"

"Probably not every time I come, but I will share with you anything significant, okay?"

"Wonderful."

13

It is time to look at some of the results of Courtney's visits with Katarina, Abie's basement spirit, and the actions which materialized as a result of these visits. I would like to remind readers once again that the words I place in conversations are not gospel because it is impossible for me to recall anything word for word after all of these years, and of course there were many conversations where my information was second hand, such as Courtney's visits with Katarina.

Courtney returned to Abie's basement the next afternoon. She decided to stick to afternoon visits for a while anyway, as that was the time of our original visit.

"Hi, Katarina," I (Courtney) called out as I popped into the basement near the staircase. Katarina was just standing there in the back, right-hand corner. She looked my way and waved to me. Of course, I waved back and slowly walked in her direction. I stopped six feet away from her, so she did not feel like she was cornered and also because that was the distance from her that she allowed me to come the previous day, before flashing me the stop sign. "Me, Courtney," I said, pointing my finger at me.

"Me, Katarina," she responded. The foreign accent had not disappeared, but I could hear her clearly.

I smiled and took a gamble. "Me, Courtney Malott," I said, pointing the finger as usual. She hesitated, and I wondered if she understood what I expected her to say.

"Me, Katarina Sosnovich," I thought she said.

"You, Katarina Sosnovich," I said, pointing my finger at her.

"Yes," she replied with a smile.

Good start, I thought to myself. Keep going. "Courtney talk English."

"Katarina talk Ukrainian, little English."

"Katarina born Ukraine?"

"Yes."

"Katarina come America on boat?"

"Yes."

"Katarina come America with husband?"

"No. Come with Mama, Poppa, Gustav."

"Gustav brother?"

"Yes."

"Katarina come America, year?"

"1953."

"How old Katarina in 1953?"

"Fifteen."

"How old Katarina now?"

"Seventeen."

"Katarina live here?" I asked, waving my hand around the basement.

"No."

"Katarina live where?"

"Concession 6."

"Katarina visit here?"

"No."

"Katarina here why?"

"Billy take here."

"Billy Katarina's friend?"

"No. Billy take Katarina."

"Katarina scream?"

"No. Billy put in mouth," she replied, placing a hand on each side of her cheek and motioning like she was tying something behind her head. "Katarina no can scream."

"What next?"

"Billy tie hands," she said turning around and placing her hands behind her lower back.

"What next?"

"Billy pick up Katarina. Put in car. Drive long time."

"Billy drove here?"

"Yes."

"What next?"

"Bring Katarina down basement. Chain Katarina bed."

At that point, Courtney concluded she was fortunate to obtain a wonderful amount of useful information. She deduced it was not the time to press Katarina for more details on her obviously unhappy captivity, so she said her goodbyes, promising to visit again soon.

That evening after our walk, Crystal and I took our usual detour into the barn for some rambunctious lovemaking. Do not get the idea that after three years of marriage, we never made love in our bedroom. Lovemaking in the bedroom was more of a slow, relaxing, and reserved coupling because we tried to be as quiet as possible. Lovemaking in our hayloft hideaway was no-holds-barred. On this particular evening we never even made it up to the hayloft before Courtney popped into the barn next to us, followed seconds later by Tom. Courtney shared with us the events mentioned above from her visit with Katarina.

"Courtney, you are marvelous," I declared. "You enticed her to reveal enough significant details that we should be able to track down her or her family."

"You have a plan, I gather?" Courtney asked.

"Oh, yes. My brother Jason's long-time best friend is a police constable in Mantle. Hopefully, he can locate Katarina in their missing persons' archives, even though she was kidnapped almost twenty years ago. I am going inside right now to call him. You and Tom can be invisible observers if you wish."

"Oh, I planned on it even without an invitation," she responded.

"Hi, folks," I said to my parents as Crystal and I entered the living room. "I need to make a phone call, but you do not need to leave." They took me at my word and continued reading. I dialed, yes, I said dialed as back in those days that was the type of phones we had, not today's modern push-button ones.

"Hello."

"Hello, would this be Rowdy Roddy Radcliff?"

It took Rod a while to stop laughing. "I haven't heard that in years. You do not sound like Jason, so I'll bet you are John Tranter."

"You're quite the detective, aren't you?"

"Maybe one day, but for now I'm still a lowly patrolman."

"I will skip the small talk, for now, Rod, but I hope you can do a little detective work for me. If I told you why, you probably wouldn't believe me at this point in time anyway, but please accept my assurance that there is a very good reason for my request, okay?"

"That's fine, John. I trust you."

"Thank you. Have you got a pen and pad?"

"I'm ready."

"Good. Back almost twenty years ago, in 1955 I believe, a seventeen-year-old Ukrainian immigrant girl went missing.

Her name was Katarina Sosnovich and she lived on the sixth concession, but I'm afraid I do not know which township that is. She spoke Ukrainian and only broken English as she was only in America a couple of years. She had a brother Gustav, but I have no names for her parents. She was apparently kidnapped. I'm afraid that is all I have for you."

"Heh, you actually have quite a bit of info there. If she is in our records, I will find her."

"Super. Please let me know when you come up with something. How are your folks doing?"

"They are happy and healthy, which is better than some. I often see your dad in town but have not seen your mom in ages. How is she making out?"

"They are both happy and healthy like your folks, thank God."

"I agree. Okay, John, I will be in touch when I have some info for you."

"Thank you, Rowdy Roddy."

"Oh, cut it out."

14

"Okay, you two, what in the world is going on?" Mom asked one second after I hung up the telephone.

Crystal and I looked at each other, but I knew it was my call. The problem was deciding just how much we could or should share with my parents. I sat down with the three of them. "Mom, do you remember way back when I was almost five that I talked one day about having a playmate in my room? You came in to get me to come to lunch, and I asked if he was staying for lunch. When we looked around my room neither of us could find him. After lunch, he returned to play with me, and you showed up again a while later to see if I was taking a nap that afternoon. I think I said I wanted to play with my new friend. We looked around the room and once again he was gone. You picked me up and plunked me down on the bed, then told me it was not nice to make up stories and you did not want to hear any more about my disappearing playmate."

"I don't think that I recall that."

"Well, this invisible friend came back many, many times. I

have been very careful, up until now, to just not ever mention it like you told me way back then. It is a rather long story, so I will just give you some of the highlights. My invisible friend was a spirit like the one that is stuck in Abie's basement. The difference between the two is that my playmate was not stuck but could pop in and out as he pleased and that is what he did in my bedroom. His name was Jason. Sometime later he brought along three other friends to play with us. Their names were Tom, Nancy, and Crystal. The spirit Jason stopped coming to play when he reincarnated as your son, who you just happened to name Jason."

Mom gasped. "You can't be serious."

"Yes, Mom, I'm dead serious. My playmate Nancy stopped coming to play when she reincarnated as your daughter, Nancy. Our playmate Crystal had already disappeared before Nancy, when she reincarnated to be my beautiful wife, but back then I never knew where she was until she reappeared after over two decades, when she applied for the vacant English job at school. That left only Tom, and he visits me often and is what is called my Spirit Guide. Okay, Crystal, your turn."

"I too had a spirit playmate when I was young. Her name was Courtney. She later brought along two friends to play with us, called June and Juliet. They stopped coming to play when they reincarnated as my twin sisters, June and Juliet. As you know we call them Junie and Julie. Courtney still visits me often and is my Spirit Guide. When I was about sixteen, my mom surprised me when she told me she knew about my invisible playmates. She added that she also had invisible playmates. Her Spirit Guide is called Mayra. Would you like to meet Courtney and Tom?"

Mom's eyes opened wide, and her jaw dropped. "Ah, okay, I guess," she hesitantly replied.

"Courtney, Tom, please show yourself," Crystal continued.

Tom materialized next to me, and Courtney did the same near Crystal.

"Hi, Mrs. Tranter. It is nice to meet you," Tom said.

Mom and Dad were in shock and just glared at the see-through spirits beside us. "Um, it is nice to meet you too, Tom," Mom replied. She looked at Courtney. "And you also, Courtney."

"Thank you," Tom replied. "Allow me to take over the story for a while. Courtney and I were present when Abie accompanied John and Crystal down to her basement yesterday, but we remained invisible just like we were until a minute ago. Abie, John, and Crystal could not see the spirit of the woman in the basement when we were there, but Courtney and I could. Abie, Crystal and invisible Courtney stood in the middle of the basement under the only light, and we all watched John walk around the circumference of the basement a couple of times. The spirit from the basement would not allow John to get close to her and would take off in a different direction whenever he came her way. When I noticed this, I also started walking around the basement like John but stayed far away from him to see if the spirit also avoided me. It did but would walk right by the three girls with no problem. I immediately deduced that the spirit was afraid of men. When the humans went back upstairs, I took off also, leaving Courtney alone with the female spirit. The rest of the story is Courtney's."

"When there was only the two of us, I slowly walked closer to the spirit, but she put up her hand to stop me when I got to about six feet from her. We had a bit of a conversation, but she spoke English with quite an accent. I began to suspect she sometimes did not understand what I was saying while speaking good English, so I resorted to hand signals and a few necessary words. I did get her name. Today I returned to Abie's basement, and we had a much longer conversation. I learned the information that your son just shared with Rowdy Roddy."

Mom smiled. "You were here for that too?"

"Oh, yes. I told Crystal and John, out in the barn a little while ago, about this afternoon's development. Tom and I followed them into the house when they came. As Spirit Guides, we pretty much shadow the person we guide, unless we are off on a mission as I was today in Abie's basement."

"Oh, so you are here a lot, then?"

"Definitely."

"Do I have a Spirit Guide too?"

"Of course. Her name is Malory. Would you like to meet her?"

"She's here too?"

"Of course. She has been shadowing you most of your life."

"Why haven't I seen her before?"

"Because you did not believe in spirits. Imagine how you would have reacted if she had materialized in front of you, the way Tom and I just did, and you knew nothing about spirits or Spirit Guides."

"I see your point."

"If you would like to finally meet Malory then just invite her to appear to you."

"Right now?"

"Right now, or anytime. You can do it in private if you prefer."

Silence reigned as all eyes were on Mom. It took her a minute or two to make a decision. "Malory, please appear here for me, or I guess, that is, us."

Malory slowly materialized over next to Courtney, not close to Mom. Mom just stared at her. I think I have mentioned before, when writing about Tom, that our Guides can appear to age along with us. Of course, I have no way of knowing if that applies to all Guides. Malory appeared to be approximately the same age as Mom. "Thank you for finally inviting me to come and visit with you."

"Sorry about that. If I had known about you earlier then I would have invited you earlier."

"I understand."

"So, I can invite you to appear anytime and talk with you?"

"Anytime."

The room fell silent for a minute, then my mom turned to my dad. "Well, Dad, are you going to hop on the bandwagon with the rest of us?"

Dad laughed. I am sure after over thirty years of marriage; this did not surprise him. "Why not. Malory, do you know my Spirit Guide?"

"Of course. We spend a lot of time together keeping an eye on you two. Your Spirit Guide is Alexander. I know he is just itching to meet you."

Dad chuckled. "Okay, Alexander, your wait is finally over. Please show yourself to us." Alexander commenced to materialize next to Tom. "Welcome, Alexander. I assume the rules for us are the same as all of the others assembled here today?"

"Absolutely," he replied.

"Great. I will certainly be calling you again soon, but for now, I need some time to digest everything that has taken place here this evening."

After another minute or two of silence, Tom said goodbye and disappeared, quickly followed by the rest of the Spirit Guides.

15

Believing she was on a roll, Courtney again visited Abie's basement the next afternoon and spoke with Katarina, relating the details to Crystal and me later in the afternoon. Here is some of the information she shared with us.

"Katarina say Billy chain Katarina to bed, yes?"

"Yes."

"Where is bed now?"

"Gone."

"Katarina like Billy?"

"No. Billy bad."

"How Billy bad?"

"Billy hit," she replied, first waving her hand across in front of my face and then making a fist and punching it towards me. She then spread her legs and pointed at her private area. "Bad here too."

"One time?"

"No. Many times or hit Katarina or bring no food."

"Katarina fight back?"

"Beginning. Tired of hit. Stop fight."

"Katarina have baby?"

"Baby here," she said, pointing to her stomach. "No have baby. Katarina sick."

"Katarina go Doctor?"

"No Doctor. Chain bed."

Courtney felt that was enough of an inquisition for one afternoon and said her goodbye, promising to return soon.

After dinner that evening, Rod Radcliff called the house and shared his research results with us. "Katarina's sixth concession address was not our township but Maris Township. (Note from me - just west of us.) Her missing person's record was noted in our files, but we did not do much actual investigating. Our file just says no evidence of foul play was discovered and she was regarded as a runaway. I called a Sergeant Stumpel in Maris and asked if his files contained more information than ours did. He asked why we were looking into this after all of these years. Of course, I did not have a reason because you did not explain your reasons to me yesterday, so I explained that the older brother of my life-long best friend asked me to look into it for him but never told me why. I assured him that you were an upright citizen, and there was no way you were doing this for improper reasons."

"Thank you for that, Rod."

"You're welcome. Sergeant Stumpel went along with my assurances and retrieved their file. The Sosnovich family was living in an old, rented house on the sixth concession. Katarina's father, Sergei, was a master baker in the Ukraine and he was employed as a baker at the largest bakery here in Maris, even though he spoke very little English. Her mother, Olga, stayed home with the two children. Katarina was fifteen and spoke absolutely no English when they arrived here in the spring, so she was never sent to school here. Little brother Gustav was sent to school. Katarina apparently loved the outdoors and would often go for walks. Maybe a quarter of a mile down their road is a fairly large bush area with a good-sized pond at the rear of it. It is called Thompson's Bush after one of its earliest owners. It is now owned by a neighboring farmer who farms the land around it but ignores the bush. The bush became a multipurpose hangout for the locals. Fishermen would walk to the back of the bush to fish in the pond. Nearby residents created walking trails through the bush. These were used by many, including Katarina. The bush was also used by the local teenagers for drinking parties on weekends.

"On the day Katarina disappeared, she went out for a walk, and her mother said she headed in the direction of Thompson's Bush, as she often did. She never came back. No evidence or witnesses were ever located to explain her disappearance. One fisherman told the Maris police, a couple of weeks after she disappeared, that he might have seen her talking with a man while on his way back to the pond to do some fishing. The two were not fighting or anything, just talking, so he did not pay much attention to them. The fisherman described the man as close to six feet tall, slim, maybe around twenty-five and wearing a baseball-style cap which pretty much covered his hair. When no evidence surfaced to explain Katarina's disappearance, the police suspected she could have run away with this or another man. They eventually classified her as a runaway and not kidnapped. They never folded their investigation for months, but they also never discovered anything to suggest she was kidnapped. Of course, Sergeant Stumpel requested that if you have information that they do not know about then to make sure you share it with them. I assured him that you would do precisely that. So, exactly what do you know about this?"

I hesitated for a few seconds, but I kind of anticipated his question and earlier worked out some possible responses. "Well, Rod, I do know much more than they apparently have in their file, but it will be better if we talk about this in person instead of over the phone. What are you doing this evening?"

"Absolutely nothing."

"Wonderful. Why don't you come over here then? Mom would love to see you."

"That's fine. See you in about fifteen."

On arrival, Rod and Mom enjoyed a warm hug. When he and Jason were in elementary school, in particular, they spent a lot of time together at one house or the other. Mom teased him at times about being her fourth child, and he would just smile. She was the one that gave him the nickname of Rowdy Roddy. He was no problem, but definitely much more active and vocal than Jason.

The five of us settled down in the living room. "There is a long story here, but I'm going to try and take some shortcuts. If you have a question, please ask. Have you seen any ghost movies or read any books about ghosts?"

"Sure, hasn't everybody?"

"You're probably right there. So, do you believe in ghosts?"

Rod contemplated that for a few seconds. "I don't know. I never really thought about it."

"I believe you. Did you ever have any playmates, before you started school, who could suddenly appear or disappear and you never could figure out where they came from or disappeared to?"

"I don't think so."

"Would you believe me if I told you that I had four of them?"

"Oh! I'm listening."

"A little friend popped into my playroom one day before Jason was even born. I thought Mom let him in, but she didn't. Over time he brought along three others. We also had lots of fun playing outside in the old barn that you know so well. Eventually, three of the four went off somewhere else. It doesn't matter where right now, so I will skip that, but one of these pop-in friends remained. His name was Tom. When I was older, he explained that he was my guide for this lifetime. He still is. Would you like to meet Tom?"

"Are you serious?"

"Tom, please show yourself." Tom began to materialize next to me.

"Holy crap. What is that?"

"Some people would call him a ghost, but because he can come and go at his leisure, he is really a spirit. Say hello, Tom."

"Hello, Rod. Its nice to finally meet you face to face."

"What do you mean by that?"

"I was hanging around John way before you ever knew Jason. I also saw you all or at least most of the time when you were here playing with Jason."

"Oh, then why didn't I see you?"

"We remain invisible when there are people present who do not know we exist. We would scare them, like in the movies, if we popped up in front of a nonbeliever. Make sense?"

"I guess so."

"Okay, Crystal. You're up next," Tom said.

"I also had three pop-in friends. Two disappeared like John's friends, but one remained. Her name is Courtney. I know you want to meet her even if you do not realize it yourself, Rod. Courtney, please show yourself to us." Courtney materialized next to Crystal.

"Hi, Rod, nice to meet you. I am the one who has been communicating with the ghost of Katarina Sosnovich, but before we go there, John needs to give you some more information."

I took over again. "Rod, you may have heard that the English Head at our school retired and I was selected to replace him. We then needed to hire another English teacher.

We picked a marvelous young lady by the name of Abigail Slaughter or more commonly called Abie Slaughter. Ever heard of her?"

"The name sounds familiar, but I am not sure why."

"She was a college all-star basketball player."

"Yes, I remember now. I have seen her on television."

"Good. She is not from around here, so she first looked for a nice apartment to rent. Not finding anything to her liking she and her dad looked for a house to buy. They found one between Promenade and Mantle. It needed some tender love and care, and she moved in the beginning of August. One evening shortly thereafter, she came down to the kitchen in the middle of the night and heard the voice of a woman in the basement crying, 'No, no, no.' She checked the basement the next morning and finding nothing out of the ordinary she telephoned here to see if we knew anyone who cleansed houses of unwelcome spirits or ghosts. I didn't tell her what we knew about spirits like Tom and Courtney, at that time, but Crystal and I went over to her house. So did Tom and Courtney, but of course, they remained invisible. We all went down to the basement. The girls stood in the center of the basement under the only light, and I walked around the circumference of the basement a couple of times but found nothing. Okay, Tom, your turn."

"I could see the spirit of this young lady in the basement. Whenever John walked towards her, she took off in another direction. I decided to walk the basement as well but nowhere near John. She would walk right by the girls but would not let John or I get close to her. I concluded that she was afraid of men so, when the humans went back upstairs, I disappeared also, leaving only Courtney down there with her. Over to you, Courtney."

"I witnessed how the ghost avoided being close to the two men. I began talking to her and stepping gradually closer to her but stopped when she put an upraised hand towards me. My goal that day was to simply try to make friends with her, so she would not be afraid of me. I quickly discovered she understood a minimum of English, so I resorted to keywords and pointing. I did get here name as Katarina and told her I would be back soon. I returned the next afternoon and acquired the information that John shared with you on the telephone last night. I visited again this afternoon and learned that someone named Billy had chained her to a bed in the basement. He raped her regularly. She fought with him at first but soon gave up fighting with him so he would stop punching or slapping her. He also would not bring her any food if she didn't cooperate. At that point, she just let him have his way with her. She got pregnant but possibly did not have the baby. She got sick and was not taken to a Doctor, so she apparently died before or during delivery. I did not think it wise to pry her for details on that experience. That is where we are with this at the moment."

"Okay, folks," Rod said, "it is now obvious that you are not making this up. Did she give you a last name for Billy?"

"No, I did not ask, and if she was kidnapped, as was apparently the case, she may not even know his last name."

I interrupted their discussion. "I have an idea. Abie has already met Courtney and Tom after our earlier visit to her basement. She asked us to keep her informed of any developments, so her knowledge is now two Courtney visits behind. If Abie is home and not very busy with anything, then I would like to telephone her and see if we can all briefly visit with her now. She needs to meet you, Rod, if you are getting involved in this investigation. Mom, Dad, you are welcome to come if you like."

16

When I telephoned Abie and told her we had an update for her but needed to deliver it in person, she said it was fine if we came over for a while. Mom and Dad declined our invitation, so we took off in two cars. Rod followed me as he knew approximately where Abie lived but could not recall specifically seeing her house as I described it to him.

"Abie, I would like you to meet Rod Radcliff. Rod, meet the famous Abie Slaughter."

"Stop that nonsense," Abie said with a grin. "It is nice to meet you, Rod," she said as they shook hands.

"I am thrilled to meet you, Abie. I watched some of your basketball games on television."

"So, you're a basketball fan, I gather?"

"Big time. You are like having a celebrity in our little towns."

"On my, I hope not. Please don't talk about my basketball escapades around town. I am hoping to keep that as low key as possible."

"If that is what you want. I hope you are not giving up

basketball altogether. After school starts, a bunch of us locals get together on Wednesday evenings at seven in your school gym for a fun game. We would love to have you join us. I live in Mantle, and I can pick you up on my way through."

"I'm sure I can find my way."

"Of course you can, but you won't know anyone. I would like the honor of introducing you to everyone, okay?"

"Are there any other women in your group?"

"Well, not at the moment. We have had two ladies join us in the past, but one quit when she became pregnant. The other one quit when she fell and broke her shooting arm, not while playing basketball, but over a curb in a parking lot. The ladies have always been welcome."

Abie grinned. "Okay, you win. I'll join."

"Super. I'll come by about six-thirty on the first Wednesday after school starts."

"I'll be ready."

At that point, I cut in on their basketball conversation. "As well as being a basketball enthusiast, Rod is also a police officer in Mantle. I have known him since he was six years old when he became the best friend of my younger brother, when they started school together."

"I will definitely be safe in his company," Abie added with a wide grin.

"That's for sure. Okay, we did not come here to talk about basketball. Rod is helping us deal with your ghost-in-the-basement problem and has already been very helpful."

"Marvelous. Let's get comfortable in the living room. I am eager to hear all about it. Can I get anyone a drink?"

Everyone passed on the drinks, and I got right down to business. "Courtney has visited with Katarina twice since we were down in your basement the other day. Katarina is revealing some interesting information to her. After Courtney's second visit I called Rod and shared the information from that visit with him. Today he contacted a police sergeant in the neighboring township, where Katarina resided. Throughout their lengthy missing person investigation, they were unable to come up with any evidence that she was kidnapped. They eventually considered her as a runaway. Courtney was back in your basement today and received more details from Katarina. I know I am skipping a lot of details right now, but she mentioned that a Billy was keeping her captive. Who did you purchase your house from?"

"Hang on. I'll go get the sales and legal documents. The name is impossible to remember." Abie was back in a minute or three. "The seller was the Estate of Frederica Consuelo Colaveccio. I was told that she passed away many years ago but left her nephew a life estate in the house. He passed away in the spring, so the house was put up for sale to complete the distribution of the proceeds from Frederica's estate."

"Who was the nephew?" I asked.

"I don't know."

"I can answer that one," Rod chimed in "Billy Colaveccio was a local drunk. He was an amazing mechanic when he was sober, but as he got older, he was rarely sober. He was only in his middle forties when he passed away in the spring, apparently due to liver failure."

"That sounds like our kidnapper to me," I said. "Crystal, will you please ask Courtney to make an appearance. I'm sure Abie would like to hear some details concerning her visits with Katarina. Abie, like you, Rod has already met Courtney and Tom."

"Courtney, please show yourself." We all watched as Courtney slowly materialized next to Crystal. "Courtney, please share with Abie the significant information that you have received from Katarina in your recent visits."

"Of course. Katarina was tied up, gagged and carried out of a bush area in a neighboring township, then driven apparently directly here by this Billy she talks about. This was all apparently preplanned as he had a bed in the basement ready to chain her to when they arrived. She says he raped her regularly, and if she would not cooperate with him, he would beat her and deprive her of any food. She eventually just let him have his way to avoid getting beaten first. If I understood her correctly, she became pregnant but never had the baby. She said she got sick and Billy never took her to a doctor. It was not clear whether she miscarried or actually died before delivery of her child. She originally arrived in America by boat from the Ukraine with her parents and brother, Gustav. That is pretty much all I know at the present time."

"Wow, I bought myself quite a house, didn't I?" Abie commented. "Have you or Tom discovered any other spirits hanging around my dream house, which is rapidly becoming a nightmare house?"

"No, there are no other spirits hanging around. If we can manage to get Katarina to cross over to our side, then you will still have your dream house. To also give you peace of mind now, I am sure Katarina will not cause any harm to you, so you really do have a dream house here. Do not stew about that, okay?"

"Okay. Thank you for clarifying that. So, what happens next, folks?"

"Tomorrow I will call Sergeant Stumpel again," Rod responded, "and bring him up to date on what you amateur detectives have uncovered so far. He will be shocked and will undoubtedly want to know how you managed to achieve, in a few days, what they were unable to accomplish over many months. That will mean, John, you need to prepare your approach for educating him on your spirit friends just like you did me and apparently Abie as well. I believe the best person to convince Katarina that she has died, and needs to cross over, is likely her brother, Gustav. Sergeant Stumpel informed me that her parents are both deceased. Hopefully, after the sergeant is educated in the ways of the spirit world, he will help us convince Gustav to pay a visit to his long-missing sister. Keep in mind this may take some time."

"That all sounds good to me," I responded, and the others all agreed with us. "I guess it is time for us to give Abie some peace and quiet before bedtime."

"I'll get back to you as soon as I get to speak with the sergeant," Rod said. "If it is okay with Abie, I will stick around a little longer and chat about basketball."

"That sounds wonderful," Abie replied.

17

R od managed to get through to the flabbergasted Sergeant Stumpel the next morning and experienced no problems convincing the sergeant to allow our group of amateur detectives to visit him in Maris. Rod was on police duty but received permission to leave the Mantle district because the journey involved a long-unsolved missing person's case. He asked me if I had any objections if he picked up Abie, if she was available, and bring her along with him to Maris. Of course, I had no objections. After all, this was her case as much as it belonged to the rest of us. I drove Crystal with me, of course. When we were all assembled in the sergeant's office and introductions were completed, he closed the door.

"I have absolutely no idea how you folks managed to solve this case in a few days when we could not solve it years ago back when Katarina's disappearance took place. I can't wait to learn how you did it," the sergeant stated eagerly.

Rod jumped in before I had a chance to respond. "First off, I need to assure you again that I have known John since I was six years old. His younger brother, Jason, has been my life-long, best friend. Jason is now a patrolman for the Kentucky State Police, but he has not been involved with this case at all. John has a Master's Degree in English and is the incoming Head of the English Department at Promenade District High School. He is totally sane, but what he is about to share with you will probably sound absolutely nuts, so I want to assure you it is the entire truth, okay?"

"I understand. Let's get on with it."

"I will skip a lot of details, but you can ask questions at any time along the way," I said. "Humans have the ability to see and communicate with the spirits of the deceased. All of us, even you, have a Spirit Guide that acts a bit like a Guardian Angel and sends us messages when we need them. I am now going to call upon my Spirit Guide to materialize here before us. Tom, please show yourself to us."

Tom slowly materialized in front of me as there was no space beside our chairs for him to do so.

"Say hello to Sergeant Stumpel, Tom."

"Hello, Sergeant. I am honored to meet you."

The sergeant glared, mouth opened wide, at the talking spirit. "Hello, Tom. Pleased to meet you too."

"We have one more Spirit Guide for you to meet, Sergeant," Tom continued.

Crystal did not miss her cue. "I have a Spirit Guide also. Her name is Courtney. Courtney is pretty much the heroine in solving this case for you, Sergeant. Katarina Sosnovich's spirit is stuck, for lack of a better word for now, in the basement of Abie's newly purchased house, which she bought from the estate of Billy Colaveccio's aunt. Billy received a life estate in the property when his aunt died and lived there until a few months ago when he passed away in his forties. When John, Abie, and I visited Abie's basement the day after she heard a female voice crying, 'No, no, no,' in the middle of the night from the basement, we could see or hear nothing unusual. Tom and Courtney accompanied us to the basement but remained unseen to the three of us because Abie knew nothing about this spirit business at the time. Katarina could see all of us, and Tom noticed that Katarina would not allow John or Tom to come close to her. When the males walked towards her, she headed off in another direction, but she showed no fear of us women. That was our first clue that Katarina's spirit was afraid of men. Courtney, please show yourself to us."

Courtney materialized in front of the closed office door, next to Crystal. "Hello, Sergeant Stumpel."

"Hello, Courtney. Before I forget to mention it later, I want to express my heartfelt appreciation for your apparently invaluable contributions towards solving the case concerning Katarina's disappearance. Please share your experiences with me."

"After the three humans and Tom left Abie's basement that day, I remained behind. My main objective was to try to make friends with the spirit so she would not be afraid to talk to me. I started off speaking to her just like I am talking with you now but quickly realized she could not clearly understand me. I switched my communications to keywords and pointing. As she spoke, I immediately noticed a foreign accent. I did establish that her name was Katarina but concentrated on convincing her I was her friend and there was no reason to be afraid of me.

"I returned the next afternoon and received some good information from Katarina, much of which was relayed to Rod that evening and to you the next day. I went back again yesterday and obtained additional information concerning her becoming pregnant. Billy had her chained to a bed in the basement and would beat her and deprive her of food if she would not submit to his sexual advances. To avoid the beatings, she submitted to his advances. She apparently never had the baby, but I am not sure whether she aborted or died before she gave birth."

"That is amazing, Courtney," the sergeant said. "I have a question unrelated to the case. How come you speak such good English?"

"Good question. When you see me, you are seeing the spirit. At the death of a body, the spirit and the soul depart the body together. It is the soul that is actually talking to you, not the spirit. The amazing secret is that souls remember everything they experienced from all of their lifetimes. I experienced two past lifetimes where I spoke English, and as Crystal's Spirit Guide this time around, I spend a lot of time around her, often unseen, so I hear numerous conversations in English. These become part of my experiences and English vocabulary. I try to talk to humans today using modern terminology, not old-fashioned expressions."

"That is certainly interesting," the sergeant stated.

"We believe that Katarina's body is probably buried in Abie's backyard," Rod piped in, "but hopefully it is possible to avoid destroying her entire backyard looking for it. We also think it would be helpful if we can get Katarina's brother, Gustav, to pay a visit to Abie's basement and hopefully be able to talk to her."

"I thought she avoided men?"

"True, but hopefully Courtney can convince her to talk to her brother. If she is going to talk to any man, it will be him. If she does talk to him, he can get the entire story of her disappearance and confinement that it may take Courtney many visits to obtain. We also hope that Gustav may be able to convince her that she has, in fact, died and maybe also assist her in transitioning to the spirit world entirely. Right now she is apparently stuck between the two worlds."

"I admit that all of this makes logical sense. I will try and speak with Gustav this evening and tell him a little of what you have shared with me, but you folks are going to have to fill him in on all of this spirit communication stuff."

"We are getting quite experienced at that," I added with a chuckle.

"I believe it," the sergeant replied. "So, is there anything else you want to tell me for now before I try to talk to Gustav?"

"Not really," I replied. "I think it would be wise if you did not mention the probability that her body is in the backyard. Let's just concentrate for now on getting him to pay her a visit."

"I agree. I also have an idea on how we may be able to determine the exact location of the body without destroying Abie's backyard. For now, I will keep that a secret and concentrate on bringing Gustav on side," the sergeant said. "All of you, please give me your telephone numbers. Gustav works in the bakery all day, so our meeting with him will probably be an evening affair."

We supplied the sergeant with our telephone numbers and bid him adieu.

18

The telephone rang while we were having dinner that evening. Mom was expecting a call, so she answered it. "John, it's a Sergeant Stumpel for you."

"Hello, Sergeant."

"Hello, John. I caught Gustav at the bakery around five this afternoon, before he went home for the day. I did not tell him much, only that some citizens have located a bit of information on his sister's disappearance. He will be in my office at eight o'clock this evening. I hope you can make it. I called Rod, but there was no answer. I did not phone Abie as she came with Rod earlier."

"Super. Crystal and I will be there for sure, and I will try to track down Rod and Abie. Thanks for getting on this so quickly."

"No thanks are necessary. Your group has pretty much solved one of our long-standing, missing person mysteries. Let's keep the ball rolling."

"I'm with you. We'll be there before eight." When I hung up the phone, I dialed Abie's number.

"Hello."

"Hi, Abbie, it's John. Sergeant Stumpel just called here. We are meeting Gustav in the sergeant's office at eight tonight. He received no answer at Rod's place."

"That's because he is here. He brought over a pizza for us for dinner. Do you want to talk to him?"

"Not necessarily, as long as he can be in Maris for eight o'clock."

"He's off duty now. We'll be there."

Crystal and I were in the parking lot at the Maris police station before seven forty-five. Rod's car pulled in before we walked to the front door of the building. Sergeant Stumpel was glad that we all arrived early.

"All that Gustav knows is that you have some information on his sister, nothing else. I will introduce all of you to him and let you proceed as you see fit."

"That's fine, I'm ready for him," I said.

Gustav arrived around eight o'clock. When the introductions were completed, Sergeant Stumpel got the meeting started. "These good folks have been looking into the disappearance of your sister for a personal reason, the details of which do not matter for the present. They are going to tell you some things which will strike you as totally unbelievable at first. When they filled me in on this, just this morning, I found all this very hard to believe at the beginning, but as things progressed it was impossible, and I do mean impossible, to deny that they were telling the truth. You will see what I mean when you hear their story; just be patient and let them finish."

"Okay, Sergeant. I will."

"Abie purchased a house out in the country over between Promenade and Mantle, a couple of months ago, after she accepted a teaching position with Crystal and me at Promenade District High School," I began. "She and her father did some cleaning and minor alterations, and she moved in a couple of weeks ago. One night she ventured downstairs in the middle of the night for a drink and heard a female voice in the basement. She hurried back upstairs where she could no longer hear the voice. In the morning, she was brave enough to venture down to the basement. The basement was almost empty and nothing appeared to have been moved around. She was afraid the house was haunted and called me to see if I knew anyone who could cleanse the house of an apparently spirit presence. At the time, she had no idea that Crystal and I knew anything about spirits. She only called us because she was new to the area and she did not know many people.

"Skipping ahead, Crystal and I have been aware for twenty years that we have Spirit Guides who assist and protect us. My Spirit Guide is called Tom and I am going to ask him now to join us here in the room. Please do not be shocked when he appears. Tom, please show yourself to us."

Tom commenced to materialize as far away from Gustav as possible. "Hello, Gustav. It is nice to meet you."

Gustav stared in silence at the see-through spirit for almost a minute. "Hello, Tom. I now understand why the sergeant warned me that this was going to be hard to believe."

"You are not alone, trust me."

"So, do I have a Spirit Guide like you also?" Gustav asked.

"Yes, everyone does."

"How come I have not seen it?"

"Because you never knew about it and never asked it to appear."

"So, if I ask it to appear now, will it do so?"

"I think so as long as you truly believe in your heart that it exists."

Gustav spent a little time apparently debating with himself whether he was ready to venture down this path. "Spirit Guide, I would like to meet you after all these years. Please show yourself to us."

A female figure about the age of Gustav began to materialize in the center of the room, facing Gustav. "Hello, Gustav. My name is Viktoria. Thank you for finally inviting us to meet."

"I would have done it earlier if I knew you were there."

"I know you would. We Spirit Guides have a lot of patience."

"So, you will show yourself to me anytime that I ask you to."

"I will. We can practice this at home, but I believe you are here this evening for another significant reason. You should continue to listen to what the others need to tell you, so I am going to disappear for now so I am not a distraction." Viktoria then began to disappear.

"That should be a big help in assisting you to believe our story," Tom said. "Crystal, please ask Courtney to join us."

"Gustav, Courtney is my Spirit Guide and has played a significant role in bringing us important information about your sister's disappearance. Courtney, please show yourself to us."

Courtney materialized next to Tom. "Hello, Gustav. I am pleased to meet you."

"Hello, Courtney. I am pleased to meet you also. I am eager to hear your news about my sister."

"Of course you are. I will skip a lot of details and try to keep this as short as possible. I met the spirit in Abie's basement. It is Katarina's spirit."

"Oh!" Gustav managed to say, his voice cracking noticeably. "Are you telling me my sister is dead? I was hoping to hear that you had found her alive."

"I am so sorry, Gustav, but yes, your sister is no longer alive. She was snatched from a bush area near your family's home back then by a man named Billy. We have learned later that this Billy lived in Abie's house for many years before Abie purchased it recently. He did not own it, but it belonged to the estate of his aunt. Billy kept Katarina captive in the basement for apparently a number of months but not years. I am aware of many more details that I can share with you, but that is not really necessary right now. Katarina died in the basement after an illness. I suspect she may have been delirious with a fever, but I have no proof of that. In any case, her spirit did not cross over upon her death to what we refer to as the other side, where Tom and I and Viktoria spend our time. This failure to cross over does not happen often. For some reason, Katarina's spirit did not cross over but became stuck in Billy's basement.

"I have visited with Katarina on three occasions now, and we have become friends. Her English is not very good, so we have some difficulty carrying on a normal conversation. It would be very helpful to your sister's spirit if you would visit with her in Abie's basement and converse with her in Ukrainian. It is important for her to understand that she does not need to remain stuck in Billy's basement but needs to cross over to our side where she will likely be eagerly met by the spirits of your parents and other deceased relatives who are there with your parents. Do you understand?"

"I think so. I need to convince her to leave the basement, but to go where?"

"Somewhere down there in the basement, or maybe outside, she should see a portal to our side. It will look like a small bright sun. I have never been a stuck spirit, so I have never gone through this. Apparently, some earthbound spirits are afraid to go near this bright light, so they stay away from it. If they would only go up close to it, they would see their relatives beckoning them to come to them, but for some reason, the relatives are unable to cross through this bright light and snatch the earthbound spirit. She has to be the one to do it. Hopefully, you will be able to convince her to walk towards the bright light and right into it. As I said, when she gets close, she will see some relatives, but she has apparently never been close enough yet to see them. Does that make sense?"

"I think so. When should we do this?"

"We can do it anytime. Katarina is stuck there, so she's always there. We can do it right now if it works for you and Abie. Okay, Abie?"

"Oh yes. She has not been a problem to me, but it will be a relief to have this taken care of before school starts next week. Are you coming with us, Sergeant?"

"Definitely. This has been my case for twenty years. I will drive Gustav, but I need directions to your place."

"I will ride with you and Gustav if that is alright," Abie said.

The three vehicles took the hour-long drive to Abie's house pretty much in tandem and the congregation reassembled in Abie's living room. "I will need to go down to the basement first," Courtney advised us. "Katarina has demonstrated a fear of men. I know you are her brother, Gustav, but you are twenty years older than you were when she last saw you. I want to prepare her ahead of time for your visit. Assuming she wants to see you, I will come back here and escort you down to the basement. She trusts me, so this should work out just fine. If she shows herself to you, you need to let me know and I will disappear to leave you two alone to chat for as long as you wish. I can always see her, so I will not automatically know if you can see her."

"I understand."

Courtney popped out of sight, and she returned about five minutes later. "All set. She is eager to see you, Gustav. She has no concept of time, so it took a while to convince her that you no longer look like her little brother. Once you start speaking to her in Ukrainian, everything should go smoothly. Are you ready?"

"As ready as I'll ever be."

Courtney and Gustav walked towards the basement door, and probably on Courtney's instructions, Gustav closed the door behind him. We waited in eager anticipation. As we waited, I remembered that the sergeant had mentioned in the morning that he had a plan to locate Katarina's body without digging up most of Abie's backyard, so I asked him about his plan."

He removed a card from his shirt pocket. "There is a renowned psychic up near Cincinnati that a number of police departments have used on occasions to locate items of evidence we cannot find, including bodies. She goes by the name Princess Summer Sparrow. I will call her later and see if she can help us out."

"How about now," Abie chimed in. "You can use my phone."

"Why not! Maybe we can catch her at home." The sergeant walked over to Abie's telephone and dialed the number.

We could not hear the conversation on the other end of the line, but I will recreate, as best that I can remember, the sergeant's part of the conversation.

"Good evening. Is this Princess Summer Sparrow?"

"My name is Sergeant Buck Stumpel with the Maris District Police Department. I talked to you about seven or eight years ago, and you helped us locate a gun that we suspected was a murder weapon. It was."

"I am delighted that you still remember helping us out on that case. Hopefully, you are willing and able to help us with a new one. We suspect there is the body of a young woman buried for some twenty years in a large back yard behind the house I am actually calling you from. We would love to know the approximate location of the body, if it actually is here, and avoid digging up much of the home-owner's yard."

"You are correct. This is not my house."

"Yes, the homeowner is here with us."

"Sure. Abie she would like to speak with you in order to help her zero in on this location."

"Hi, Princess. This is Abie. I am the new homeowner."

"Yes, there is an earthbound spirit in the basement. Her brother is down there now with her attempting to assist her to cross over."

"Yes, we believe the body in the backyard belonged to the earthbound spirit."

"Yes, there is also the Spirit Guide of a friend of mine, who is also present here with us now, down in the basement as well. The Spirit guide – her name is Courtney – has been able to befriend our earthbound spirit and obtain some valuable information from the earthbound spirit."

"Her name is Katarina Sosnovich. She was a Ukrainian immigrant, only in our country about two years before she was kidnapped and brought here twenty years ago by the previous resident of my new house."

"Okay, I am listening."

"That is wonderful and definitely easy for me to remember. You are sure Courtney will be able to do this?"

"Sorry, I do not doubt you. This is all new to me."

"Thank you very much for your assistance with this. It means a lot to me to have Katarina cross over to where she belongs and no longer residing in my basement."

"Thanks again. Would you like to speak with Sergeant Stumpel again?"

"Okay, I will do that. I really appreciate this. Bye, Princess."

Abie hung up the phone and returned to her chair. "Princess says goodbye, Sergeant, and it was nice to speak with you again."

Courtney picked that moment to materialize with us. "Excellent timing, Courtney," Abie said. "Sergeant Stumpel phoned a psychic that helped him a number of years ago. She later asked for the homeowner, and she proceeded to give me the directions for how you can proceed to locate the body in my backyard. She insists you can handle this. You are to go to the center of the backyard, then walk back and forth to and from the extended house lines. Billy buried her behind the house so no one driving by could see him doing it. It is not directly behind the middle of the house but fairly close to the middle. As you turn each time at a house line, you need to move closer to the house. She says you will know it when you are standing on top of the body."

"That sounds pretty clear," Courtney replied. "Who is responsible for overseeing the digging process?"

"That honor belongs to Rod as I have no jurisdiction over here in your township," Sergeant Stumpel stated.

"That's correct," Rod confirmed. "The Chief already knows that this could happen anytime, and he has his people on alert. I will make some calls tonight, or first thing in the morning if we know it is a go. Who plans to join us?"

Everyone, including Sergeant Stumpel, planned to be there.

"So, Courtney, how did things go in the basement?" I asked.

"Pretty good. Even though I explained to Katarina that Gustav would not look like he did twenty years ago, she still showed some reluctance in believing he was really her brother. As soon as he started speaking Ukrainian to her, she was okay with him. When they were talking away like long lost friends, I disappeared and joined you up here. Before I forget, I think it is probably best if we do not let Gustav know we are going to dig up his sister's remains in Abie's backyard tomorrow. I am sure it would be hard on him to be present throughout the proceedings. Sergeant, you can tell him the results later after the fact, okay?"

"Excellent idea," he responded.

We probably chatted for almost fifteen minutes before we heard the door to Abie's basement open and then close. Gustav shuffled into the living room in a daze, tears running down his cheeks. Crystal jumped up and tore over to him. They hugged each other tightly for a couple of minutes, but it probably felt much longer to the rest of us. Finally, Gustav let go of his bear hug on Crystal and she followed suit. Gustav wiped his cheeks with his fingers and looked around at us. "I'm sorry, everyone. This has been really tough on me. Katarina has now crossed over, and she was met by our parents. I could not see them, but she excitedly called to them, so I have no doubts that they were there to welcome her. I want to thank all of you for making this miracle happen. A mere few hours ago, I would never have dreamed that any of this could even take place. I have a lot to learn about spirits, but I am determined to learn as much as I can. It is nice to have discovered Viktoria to assist me on this new journey. You are all Angels to me."

Crystal had tears trickling down her cheeks. My eyes were glassy. Up to that point, our objective had been to cleanse Abie's basement of an unwanted spirit. Probably all of us were so overpowered by Gustav's comments that we realized the true value of this unlikely adventure was for Gustav's soul to finally feel at peace knowing his long-lost sister was now in good hands.

Sergeant Stumpel took this opportunity to stand and walk over to Gustav, giving him a quick hug. "Let's go home, Gustav."

With their departure, Courtney took charge. "Okay, detectives, we are not finished yet. Let's go out back and see if we can locate a body that has been missing for twenty years."

It was after ten o'clock by then, but we had a clear sky and an almost full moon, so we did not bother to collect the flashlights that Abie offered to round up around her house. Before Courtney walked to the approximate center of the back yard, she instructed Rod and I to bring six boulders from the rock pile in the back corner of the deep yard, which we proceeded to do. After approximately ten turns at the extended house lines, she slowed down and then stopped. She then zig-zagged back and forth over a small area. "I have found her." She then instructed Rod and I as to where we were to place our rock collection, which turned out to be a coffin-sized rectangle.

Back inside Abie's house, Rod called his police chief, even though it was almost eleven o'clock. "Hi, Chief, it's Rod. I'm sorry to call you so late, but I wanted to let you know that we have determined the exact location of the body of our missing young lady." Rod listened for a minute. "Thanks for setting everything up ahead of time. Nine o'clock in the morning sounds good if you can make it work. I'll meet them at the station and bring them over here. See you in the morning."

After Rod hung up the phone, he turned to us. "There is an archeology club in Promenade that has a lot of experience digging up old suspected sites where Native Americans camped on hunting expeditions to this area. They are very precise in what they do. We have used them to carefully recover buried bodies in the past, and the Chief went ahead and potentially lined them up for tomorrow morning to come here and demonstrate their skills."

19

Crystal and I arrived at Abie's house before eight-thirty the next morning. Abie was sitting out front in a lawn chair. She offered us a coffee, and we eagerly accepted, even though we chugalugged one earlier at breakfast. It was a beautiful, sunny August morning at that hour but was supposed to turn quite warm by afternoon. Around nine-fifteen, Rod's police cruiser and two other vehicles turned into the driveway. After Rod introduced the seven members of the archeological club to us, he took them around the side of the house to where the action would soon begin. I knew two of the club members from Mantle. One was the father of a former student of mine. The other was a retired nurse my mother had known since grade school. Abie, Crystal, and I followed them around to the backyard. This recovery procedure was new to all of us. We were determined to watch it unfold, although the girls were uncertain whether they were prepared to remain there after the body was discovered.

One of the group members used a long knife to slice through the grass and down to the grass roots, just inside the lines of the six rocks Rod and I placed there ten hours earlier. He then divided the cut portion of lawn into four pieces, which measured about a foot and a half by three feet. Another member took a flat shovel and slipped it under the sod to loosen it up. The four pieces of soil were then rolled up and placed on a corner of a plastic tarp that they had brought with them. The rolls of sod looked exactly like the ones we see on the sod trucks that are delivering them to new homes after the construction projects are primarily completed. I mentally noted that our recovery group was certainly experienced and careful. At that point, Sergeant Stumpel joined our little congregation of curious spectators.

The project supervisor retrieved three miniature rakes out of their toolbox. He handed them to two ladies and the student's father that I knew from Mantle. The tines on the mini rakes were only about half an inch long and the handle probably a foot long. After the two rocks were moved out of the way from the center of the rectangle, the three rake recipients knelt down, two of them on one of the long sides of the grassless plot and the third on the opposite side between the two. They gently raked at the dirt directly in front of them. The dirt was not soft and loose, but it was also not packed down and really hard. After they loosened the dirt down about two or three inches and piled it up in front of them, the supervisor gave each of them a bucket so they could pick up the loose dirt with their gloved hands. They handed the buckets to the three workers who were watching and waiting. The buckets were dumped in the center of the large tarp, and then returned to the rakers and the process was repeated.

"Very few people bury bodies close to the surface, or really, really deep," the supervisor told us. "They are generally in a rush to get the dastardly deed done before someone sees them. When we get close to a foot deep, where many bodies are located, the rakers will ditch the rakes and switch to brushes. Our goal at first is to locate the body without damaging. Note that our helpers selected positions over what is probably the victim's knees, hips, and upper chest. They will not bother with the rest of the dirt over the body until we find out how deep down it lies."

It made good sense to me. One rake clanged against something hard, and the other rakers immediately stopped raking. It turned out to be a stone about an inch and a half in diameter. The lady pitched it over on the tarp and work recommenced. When they were down probably nine or ten inches deep, the workers changed to a much gentler raking stroke. "I think I just hit something," the gentleman shouted, and the ladies immediately stopped raking. The man gently moved dirt towards him with his hands until he had much of the loose dirt out of the way. He then slowly worked his fingers into the remaining dirt where he apparently thought his rake had contacted something hard. "I think I have a hip bone," he declared.

The supervisor turned to us spectators. "Okay, folks, I think it is time for curious spectators to leave us to complete our work. Memories of watching bodies being recovered can sometimes haunt spectators for decades. Rod and the sergeant can stay, but it is best that the rest of you go out front and wait this out. Rod can visit you off and on to share updates."

"Thank you for allowing us to watch the procedure this long," I said, and the girls and I walked around to the front where we settled down into lawn chairs.

"Can I get you guys a drink?" Abie asked, but before we could answer her, a car zipped along the driveway towards us.

As soon as he hopped out of his car with a camera dangling from his neck and hustled towards us, I recognized him. "The press has arrived." I waited for him to reach us. "Ladies, please welcome Dirk Shattenkirk, the roving reporter for the *Promenade Free Press*. Dirk, you may have already met my wife Crystal, and now meet Abigail Slaughter, our new English teacher at Promenade District High School."

"Pleased to meet you, ladies," Dirk replied. "I hope I have the correct house where the archeological club is assisting the police to recover a body."

"This is the place. They are around back," I replied.

"Thanks," Dirk said and hurried off.

"How come he gets to be present when we were politely removed from the action scene?" Crystal asked.

"Reporters have special privileges, right, Abie?"

"Oh, yes. Their job is to gather and spread the news. How did Dirk know all this was going on? Did Rod tell him?" Abie asked somewhat perturbed?

"Probably not. Dirk's sister is the secretary at the Mantle police station. Everyone there probably knows this is going on. She makes sure her brother is advised where the excitement is so he can do his job."

"Should she be doing that?" Crystal asked.

"If it is not something that is confidential, then the public has a right to know. Katarina's missing person case has been public knowledge for twenty years."

"I guess that makes sense," Crystal replied.

A half an hour or so later, Dirk came around the house and joined us in the front yard. "Is it alright if I occupy the vacant lawn chair for a few minutes?"

Abie did not respond, so I finally broke the silence. "Of course, Dirk."

"Thank you."

"I got a lot of information from Rod and Sergeant Stumpel, but I would appreciate it if you folks could elaborate a little on what is taking place here and how it all came about. Abie, I thought I recognized you when John introduced you, so I asked Rod if you were, in fact, the college all-star basketball player. He told me you were trying to keep a low profile and to tell you he only confirmed my assumption was correct because he could not lie to me."

Abie grinned. "Okay, I guess I won't hold it against him. Can you leave the basketball part out of your article on the recovery of the body, please?"

Dirk sighed. "Unfortunately, I would not be doing my job if I did. You may not realize it, but you are the biggest news that has happened in these parts in some time, even bigger than the recovery of the remains of the suspected Katarina Sosnovich, who almost everyone in these parts has long forgotten about."

"Pretty please. I'll sign a souvenir basketball for you."

"Dang that is tempting, but my job must come first. You have probably talked with dozens of reporters throughout your basketball years, and I am sure you have learned that most of us are conscientious and dedicated individuals. I am. Please don't hold it against me that I need to do my job."

Abie's frown quickly changed to a smile. "Okay, I certainly understand your dedication to the job."

"Of course you do. You know all about dedication, right?"

"You got me there."

"Now that we have that settled, will you answer some questions for me, please?"

"I won't promise all, but some."

Dirk laughed. "That's fair. Okay, what brought you to the Mantle-Promenade area in the first place?"

"I want to be an English teacher in High School. I grew up in a rural area, and then went to College in a big city, as you undoubtedly know. I'm not a big city person, so I concentrated on applying for vacant English positions in rural areas. Promenade District High School was the first place that invited me in for an interview. John's three-man committee apparently liked my qualifications enough to offer me the vacant position."

Dirk finished scribbling his notes. "Good. How did you end up in this house?"

"I looked around for a nice apartment to rent and could not find anything I really liked. My father decided to take me house hunting. This house, on a quiet road out in the country, reminded me of home. We looked at it, noticed that it needed a little work and tidying up, but it was structurally sound. We made an offer, and it was accepted. My dad then helped me – actually, that should be I helped my dad spiff it up. I moved in the beginning of August, and I love it here."

"Neat. Okay, how did you know there was a body in the backyard?"

"Did Sergeant Stumpel tell you he called a psychic for assistance?"

"Yes."

"Good. You need to quiz him on that then."

"I already have." Dirk turned his attention to me. "How did you and Crystal become involved in all of this?"

"Being new to this area, Abie hardly knows anyone, and we have known her since the day we hired her. I guess we can say she felt better going through this with some friendly company."

Dirk thanked us for our cooperation and took off minutes before Rod joined us out front. "They are pretty much done until they remove the skeletons." That caught all of off guard. Rod grinned. "There is the skeleton of a baby lying just above her hip bones. Courtney's information appears to be right on. I have to radio in and get them to bring over a cheap coffin, so the bones can be removed and carefully reassembled in it for transporting to the station. I assume a coroner will need to inspect the remains, but that is certainly not my job. You guys might as well go to lunch. There is not going to be much more news today," he said and headed for his cruiser.

"I am glad now that we did not watch the recovery of the

bodies," Crystal said. "Seeing the skeleton of the baby would have done me in."

"Me to," Abie added.

"How about I treat you two lovely ladies to a pizza lunch in town?" I asked.

"That's a brilliant idea," Crystal replied.

20

The weekly edition of the *Promenade Free Press* was delivered to subscribers and newsstands on Friday morning, the Friday morning before the beginning of the new school year. It propelled Promenade and Mantle residents into frenzy. The entire front page was devoted to the discovery and recovery of the body suspected of being the long-missing Katarina Sosnovich, buried behind the house formerly occupied by the late Billy Colaveccio. (Keep in mind that this was way before today's DNA testing was perfected.) For the public record, the case file showed that the body was suspected to be that of Katarina and was discovered with the assistance of a psychic from the Cincinnati area. No mention is made of any spirit communications. Gustav Sosnovich later claimed the remains and had them buried in a plot next to their parents.

The local frenzy was not the result of the discovery of the body. Well over half of the front-page article was devoted to the current owner of the Colaveccio house, Abie Slaughter, the Promenade-Mantle area's first-ever high-profile celebrity. No one cared that she was not born and raised here. Way more significant than born and raised here was the fact that she chose to live and work here and that was all the locals needed to claim her as their own. Dirk researched her high school and college accomplishments on the basketball courts and shared them with the world – well, at least the local world. In one day, the I-want-to-fly-under-the-radar Abie became the town hero. I guess that's heroine. If there was an election for mayor that week and she ran, she would have won in a landslide.

Fortunately, she had a weekend to adjust to her once-again celebrity status. At school on Monday, when the principal introduced her as our only new staff member that year, she received a standing ovation. A very long, resounding, standing ovation. She turned beet red but smiled from ear-to-ear. The principal almost needed to drag her to the microphone to say hello to the students. Her voice cracked as she fought valiantly to hold back a flood of tears, but fortunately, the applause was still ringing through the gymnasium, which doubled as our auditorium as well, so at first, no one could actually hear her except some of us teachers close to her up on the stage.

Abie motioned to the student body to sit back down. As they gradually abided by her wishes, the applause quickly subsided until the gymnasium fell silent. She had her emotions under control by then, fortunately. She thanked the students profusely for their warm and unexpected welcome. She added that she sincerely looked forward to meeting them individually as the school year progressed and that she was thrilled she selected Promenade as the town to begin her hopefully long and successful career as an English teacher. With that, she left the microphone and returned to her chair between Crystal and me.

At the end of the first day, Crystal and I were eager to hear how Abie's day went. Her one-word response was fantastic. We knew right then that she would have no problems. She told us that Maggie Farnsworth, the girls basketball coach, corralled her at some point and confided that she was eager to start a family this fall. She begged Abie to take over the basketball team from her. Abie happily agreed to do so.

From day one, the school year progressed pretty much normally. Abie fit right in with the rest of the staff. Now it was Crystal's turn to spring a surprise on me. She sheepishly told me in November that she finally wished to stop taking her birth control pills but would not do so if I objected. I had been encouraging her to make this move for a couple of years, so I danced around like a five-year-old on Christmas morning. I deliberately used that example. On Christmas morning, the Christmas card attached to my Christmas present from Crystal read, "Merry Christmas Daddy-To-Be."

Charlotte Marie Tranter was born the following September. When Crystal was born, her mother, Cassandra, decided to start what she hoped would become a family tradition by giving her first-born daughter a name starting with the letter C. Crystal advised me of this months before the birth and also that she planned to follow her mother's tradition. She chose to call our first-born Charlotte, or John, after me, if he was a boy. I had no objections to either choice.

Maggie Farnsworth, the former girls' basketball coach, also managed to become pregnant, even before Crystal, and gave birth in August to a handsome young fellow she called Brad. Both ladies requested a one-year leave of absence from the school board. Their requests were granted, so we needed to hire two teachers who would know their teaching position could possibly be only for one year. Maggie was a science teacher, so I was only involved in the hiring of an English teacher for the second year in a row. Abie turned out to be a much better choice than we even dreamed she could be. That milestone would be hard to beat. We were well prepared for the possibility that the new, temporary hire could not likely be such a pleasant surprise as Abie. While I have Abie on my mind, I want to mention that Rod and Abie began dating soon after the school year started and became engaged in July before Charlotte was born.

Going back to our challenge of finding a replacement English teacher for Crystal, our principal came up with a brainwave. Nancy Rutledge was the teacher I replaced when I first was hired at Promenade High because she was pregnant and obtained a leave of absence for one year. She then extended it for a second year. I do not believe it was an actual written policy, but the school board apparently followed the practice of not granting a leave for more than two years. The leave recipient was therefore forced to decide whether she wished to return after the two years or resign her position. Nancy chose to resign, and her position became officially, not temporarily, mine. I had been casually acquainted with her, but our principal and his wife were quite good friends with Nancy and her husband. Our principal mentioned to me that he thought she might be interested in filling in for Crystal, as her children were now in school full time, so he was not going to advertise the vacancy until he asked her if she was interested in it. She was but asked for a few days to mull it over. She agreed to come back and join our merry staff. It really was a merry staff. We had no rabble-rousers who delighted in creating conflicts.

In the spring after Charlotte was born, the school board contacted Crystal and asked her to confirm that she was returning for the next school year, or if she wished to continue her leave, then she needed to formally request a one-year extension. It sounds so formal, but apparently the board needs to assert its right to say yes or no and not to have teachers assume it is automatically granted. Financially, we were sound, living rent-free with my parents, so I told her to do whatever she wanted to do. She applied for the second year's leave, and it was granted. That presented a new problem, or actually I should refer to it as an option, instead of a problem. The dilemma was whether we were ready to try for baby number two or postpone it for a while. Once again, I told Crystal it was her decision to make. She talked it over with my mom and thought about it for a week or so and then stopped taking her birth control pills once more.

Nancy was asked if she was prepared to fill in for Crystal at school for a second year and she said sure, once again nullifying the need for us to go teacher hunting to fill a one-year position. Johnathan Jason Tranter was born in November. Instead of having two John's in the house, we decided to call him Jay-Jay. Spring is not too far away from November, so now we had the toughest decision to make. Was Crystal prepared to resign her position, with no guarantee of ever getting back into Promenade High, or did she want to leave her two babies in the care of my mother. Mom was still pretty spry for a fifty-nine-year-old. She assured us she could handle it and would do so willingly. I emphasized to Crystal that she had to decide what she wanted to do in her heart, and there would be no financial problems for us getting by on one salary. After a mother-to-mother talk with Nancy, who had gone through the same gut-wrenching dilemma, Crystal decided to resign her position and enjoy her children's early years, at least until they were both in school. Nancy was offered Crystal's permanent position, and she took it.

I know that this is a lot of baby talk, but babies were the highlight of those years. We are not done yet. Abie and Rod got married back in the summer after they were engaged one year. The wedding took place in Abie's hometown, and it was a magnificent affair. Of course, Crystal and I were invited. After Abie and Rod started dating, they became the couple in our quiet social circle that Crystal and I spent the most time with. If it sounds like I am bouncing all over the place with this story, be patient. It will all tie in. By this time Kindergarten existed in all of our district's elementary schools. Charlotte started Kindergarten when she was five and Jay-Jay would begin the next year. Abie managed to become pregnant in late November of Charlotte's kindergarten year, resulting in her requesting a leave of absence for the year Jay-Jay started kindergarten. It was granted, and the principal and I were delighted to have Crystal fill Abie's position and rejoin us back at Promenade High. Crystal and I asked Abie numerous times if she deliberately allowed her first pregnancy to occur the year that both of our children were in school. She would only smile and tell us, "You'll never know."

21

The previous chapter covered a number of years, but I wanted to demonstrate, in particular, how the arrival of the next generation and the teacher shuffles in my English department seemed to be coordinated by the Powers Above, which I certainly believe to be true.

Now, I need to elaborate on some of the events that occurred over those years. First off, I will do something I have kind of avoided up until now, but which will probably assist readers in understanding some of the decisions we made along the way – stating our ages.

If you check back to Chapters One and Two you will see that Crystal and I are almost six and a half years apart in age. I was born in the late spring, and the spirit Crystal disappeared from my life for over two decades, in the late fall. When Crystal and I married in July, I was thirty-one and she was twenty-four. Four years later we were blessed with our daughter Charlotte, in September. I was now thirty-five and Crystal was twenty-eight. Fourteen months later, Jay-Jay arrived. I was thirty-six and Crystal just turned thirty. Charlotte started kindergarten a little before her fifth birthday. I was now forty and Crystal was thirty-three. Jay-Jay started school and Crystal returned to teaching at Promenade District High School a year later. You can do the math.

Going back to Abie's pregnancy leave, there was an unusual complication that we needed to sort out. Abie coached the girls basketball team from her arrival at Promenade High. The team was quite successful, probably primarily due to Abie's coaching and experience, but they could never manage to win a championship. Unfortunately, to that point, we were never blessed with a star player of Abie's caliber. The team's success was the result of hard work. Our principal teased Abie before she applied for her leave of absence, telling her that he would ask the school board not to grant her a leave of absence if she did not agree to continue coaching the girls' team while on leave. He was only teasing, of course, so he then begged her to continue in her coaching position. Abie did not put up a fight at all.

I mentioned earlier that after Abie and Rowdy Roddy began dating, they quickly became the best friends of Crystal and me. They were regular visitors in our home. Mom adored Abie like she did Crystal, and Mom and Dad and I had known Rod most of his life. The complication I mentioned above involved locating a babysitter for Abie's yet unborn bundle of joy during basketball season. Basketball games and practices are nothing like most workdays. They have little regularity, and Abie was unable to locate a desirable sitter who would commit to watching the baby whenever Rod was not home to do so. Mom came to the rescue, as moms do. She loved having Charlotte and Jay-Jay underfoot during the years before they started school, even though Crystal was also there with her. Abie did not want to impose on Mom like that, but it is hard to win an argument with Mom, trust me, so it was settled. The two ladies agreed that Abie would let Mom know the evening before, or earlier, if the baby would be arriving the next day and approximately when.

Rod did not really want the baby boy called Roderick Junior, so Abie partially named him after her father. Norman Roderick Radcliff arrived in September. He was adorable. Crystal, Charlotte, Jay-Jay and I were often home when Mom was babysitting, so in reality, he often had five babysitters. Spoiled or what! Rod was very cooperative in this arrangement. If he was working days, he would come and pick up Normie, as the little guy immediately became affectionately known, after his shift ended instead of leaving him with us until Abie was finished with her basketball duties. If Rod was on the afternoon shift, one of them would drop Normie off and Abie would pick him up later.

Back to Charlotte and Jay-Jay. Because they were only fourteen months apart, they virtually grew up together and usually played together, except when there were occasional disagreements. One day, shortly after Charlotte started school, Crystal and Mom were watching out the window while Jay-Jay was playing in the back yard. The two ladies both intuitively felt that he was playing with someone they could not see. Now that Mom, Dad, Crystal and I were knowledgeable about Spirit Guides and communicated with ours regularly, we were always on the lookout for signs that our children or grandchildren also had invisible friends. There were never any incidents, over the years Charlotte and Jay-Jay were both home, when any of us felt they were playing with invisible friends, so this was a first that day.

When Jay-Jay came in for lunch, Crystal asked him who he was playing with. He told her Robbie. She asked where Robbie lived, and he said he did not know and that he just showed up to play a few days earlier. The delighted ladies asked no further questions.

I later asked Tom if Charlotte had invisible friends we never noticed.

"No."

"Why not?"

"With Charlotte and Jay-Jay playing together so often, it was not practical for invisible friends to visit with her on the rare occasions she was not with Jay-Jay."

"Does she have a Spirit Guide?"

"Of course."

"What is her Spirit Guide's name?"

"I can't tell you."

"Why not?"

"That is Charlotte's private information."

"Aw, come on."

"You need Charlotte's permission first."

"She's only five years old."

"I suspect someday you will eventually get your answer."

22

Otto Obagato was hailed as Nigeria's greatest basketball star. He was six feet, eight inches tall and built like a football player. Even though the Nigerian basketball team was not competitive in the IAAF World Championships, the professional scouts were greatly impressed with Otto's potential. A number of teams were interested in signing him. In his third season in the NBA, he and an opponent were involved in a devastating collision. Otto suffered major injuries to his right knee. His season was over. He attempted a comeback the next season, but the knee would not hold up under the rigors of competition in the world's premier league. His playing career was cut short.

The scout, who was responsible for his original signing to a professional contract, suggested that he apply for a vacant position with an Ivy League University, scouting boys high school basketball players. Otto and his recent bride, Marvita, did not wish to return to Nigeria, so he applied for the vacant position and was hired. This all took place a number of years in the past. His scouting territory included Promenade District High School, so he watched numerous boys' basketball games in our gym over the years. Of course, he remained a dedicated basketball fan and followed the men's and women's college teams as well as the NBA teams, now primarily on television.

Through the years before her leave of absence, Abie tried to attend as many of the boys' basketball games as she could fit into her schedule when they were played at Promenade High. She had noticed Otto in attendance now and then and simply assumed he was one of the numerous scouts who showed up for the high school games throughout the season. They had never actually met. One day, just after Abie requested her leave of absence, he showed up at her girls' game. He was hard to miss. Abie noticed him and wondered why he was attending a girls' game all of a sudden, but quickly shifted her attention back to the task at hand. Abie's girls snuck a five-point victory over the first-place team, through superior determination and Abie's innovative coaching techniques which the opponent was apparently unprepared to counter.

Otto was standing outside our girls' dressing room with a number of parents, waiting to take their victorious heroines home. All of the players and parents were gone when Abie finally emerged from the girls' physical education office and coaches' room, which was located next to the change room. She was startled to find Otto there.

He introduced himself and apologized for startling her. "Would it be possible for us to talk for a few minutes, Abie? You can pick any location you would like. I do not want you to feel fearful for your wellbeing."

Abie grinned. "I have seen you at our boys' games now and then and figured you were one of the scouts. I was a little surprised when I spotted you at our game today. I am okay with talking right here if you are."

"This is fine, thank you. I have talked to numerous scouts

over the past couple of years concerning who is the best girls' basketball coach in this area. Most of them voted for you. I watched a number of your college basketball games on television. I know all about your talents as a player but knew very little about your coaching skills. By the way, that was a great coaching job you pulled off today, young lady."

Abie chuckled. "Thank you. I figured if we let them dictate the way we played the game, we would probably lose miserably, so I worked at using an old system which most coaches have forgotten about, if they ever knew about it at all. I was thrilled that it worked in our favor."

"It certainly did. Okay, I am sure you are eager to go home so I will get right to the point. My family lives in a neighboring township. I have a daughter in grade eight. She seems to have inherited my physical stature and also some of my basketball skills. My scouting experience tells me that she may possess the abilities to become a successful college basketball player. She needs the best coach around to develop her natural talents in high school, so she gets scouted by the colleges, just like you were. I am sure you are the person I am looking for."

"Because she is out of our district, she cannot go to school here."

"I know that, but we can move here."

"You would do that?"

"Yes. I travel around a lot, so it does not matter that much where I live. My wife and I have agreed that we will move to wherever our daughter will receive the best high school coaching."

"That is great. I would love to have her here but don't see why you needed to tell me ahead of time."

"We do not want to uproot the entire family and move here if you have any plans to transfer to other schools. Do you figure you will continue to teach and live here?"

Abie bit her lip.

"Oh, oh," Otto said with a startled look on his face.

Abie grinned. "Can you keep a secret?"

"Oh, yes."

"I am pregnant and going on a leave of absence next year, but the principal arm-twisted me into promising I would continue coaching the girls' team while on leave. I loved the idea. My husband is a police constable here in Promenade, so we are likely destined to be lifetime residents in the area."

"That's a big relief. I do not expect you to do her any favors but hopefully push her to reach her full potential."

"It sounds like she could be the star player that our school has never had in the past. I look forward to working with your daughter. What is her name, by the way?"

"Amieann, one word, not two. Amieann Obagato." Otto took a couple of cards out of his pocket. "These are my cards. Tuck one away, please, and if you do not mind could you please write your home telephone number on the other one for me."

Abie took the cards and searched her purse for a pen. Otto quickly removed one from his pocket and held it out near her purse.

Abie grinned. "I know I have one or two in here, but sometimes when I need something, it is like finding a needle in a haystack." Abie wrote down her telephone number for Otto and handed him the card and his pen.

"Thank you," he said. "I will get in touch with you now and then to keep you updated on our moving progress. We will probably soon start looking for houses in your area but will not move Amieann and her younger brothers before the school year is completed."

"Good. Education is important, too."

"Oh, I know it. Thanks for your time and answers. I hope

your team has a successful season and a long run in the playdowns."

"Thank you."

Otto turned and walked towards the front doors and the guest parking lot. Abie headed for the side door and the staff parking lot.

ABIE DIALED – yes, it is still before cell phones – Otto's home telephone number.

"Hello."

"Hello, Mrs. Obagato. Could I speak with Otto, please?"

There was a little giggle. "It's Amieann, not my mom. I will call my dad."

"Hello."

"Hello, Otto, it's Abie Radcliff from Promenade District High School. Are you still looking to move your family into our district for the next school year?"

"Definitely. We have been looking around for the right house but have not yet come up one we really liked."

"Good, I think. On the drive home from school today, I noticed a for sale sign on a really nice house about one mile before our house. I go by there twice a day and never noticed the sign before, so I'm pretty sure it is a new listing. It is owned by a good family I have known since I arrived in Promenade. Their youngest daughter was on my basketball team for her last two years of high school. She was good but not good enough to make her college basketball team. Sorry, I'm digressing. As I said, it is a pretty nice house, and there is a bonus. They have a rather large cement parking lot at the side of the house with a regulation size basketball net at one end. Do you think you might be interested in a place like that?"

"Absolutely. Have you got some contact information?"

"Oh yes."

"Hang on a sec while I grab a pen and paper."

Otto and his wife checked out the house the next day, loved it, and made an offer close to the asking price. It was accepted, and that is the story of how the fortunes of Promenade High's girls' basketball team were changed forever.

23

I know! By now you are probably wondering what this is all about. Don't go away; you are about to find out.

At the beginning of July, the Obagato family moved into their new home. It was situated on the same road and about one mile north of Abie's home. Abie quickly became their go-to contact in this new township where they hardly knew anyone else. Abie relished her new position as premier contact for the family and the opportunity it afforded her to better get to know Amieann. Every morning during summer vacation, weather permitting, Otto and Amieann were out on their treasured, half-basketball court beside the house, practicing moves and shots. Amieann's younger brothers, Derrick and Dwight, often joined them but soon got bored and took off to investigate their two-acre property with a bush and a small pond behind the house.

Some mornings, the very pregnant Abie would drive to the Obagato home and settle into a comfortable lawn chair to observe the proceedings. Often Marvita, two ice teas in hand, would join her to watch the basketball wizardry on display in front of them. Otto was then over forty, a bit out of shape, a little overweight and had a gimpy knee, all of which helped demote him to the second-best basketballer on the court. Abie told Crystal and I, a few weeks after she started watching the father and daughter impressing their meager spectator crowd, that she was sure Amieann was a more developed basketball player at fourteen than she herself had been at that age.

When the new school year started, Amieann landed in Crystal's grade nine English class. We had met and spent time with the Obagato family on a number of occasions throughout the summer, so Amieann and Crystal were well acquainted by then. Norman Roderick (Normie) Radcliff arrived near the end of August. Amieann adored him. Actually, we all did.

With the beginning of the new school year, the old-timers' Wednesday evening basketball nights commenced at Promenade High. Rod and Abie had participated regularly after Abie first arrived in Promenade. Rod went back for the start of the new season, but Abie postponed her arrival for a while. She wanted to allow her body to completely heal after a difficult delivery and she was breast-feeding Normie, giving her two good reasons to delay her return to the courts.

Abie did a little conniving, though. She wanted to see Amieann in action before the high school basketball practices commenced in November. She asked Rod to check with some of the old-timers to see if they objected to a unique fourteen-year-old joining their ranks. The reception was mixed. It had not been done in the past, and some group members were concerned that they would be setting a precedent for opening their group up to all of the high school students who wanted to participate. When Abie broached the topic with Otto, he put the kibosh on her brainwave anyway, reminding Abie that he did not want anyone to suspect Abie was giving Amieann extra privileges because they were now neighbors and good friends. Amieann viewed Abie as the big sister she never had.

Tryouts and regular practices commenced in November as usual. The fourteen-year-old Amieann outshone everyone and was destined to become a starting forward. Many of her teammates envisioned a championship title down the road and were happy to inherit this extremely talented new star. A few of the not-so-talented seniors were not so enthusiastic because they quickly recognized the fact that there playing time was about to be diminished.

After the team for the new season was selected, Abie prepared the reduced squad for the season opener just around the corner. Amieann rode the school bus to and from school, except on practice afternoons when Abie would drive her neighbor home so Amieann's parents did not need to pick her up after practice like the other parents did. One practice just before their first game, Amieann had a totally unanticipated, worse-than-lackluster performance which shocked everyone. A couple of teammates ribbed her about it a few times, but Abie silently observed the situation and attempted to speculate what in the world had caused this unacceptable turn-around. That changed on their drive home.

"Okay, kiddo, what is going on? You were terrible today, you know?"

"I'm sorry," Amieann whispered, fighting back tears.

"Please tell me what's bothering you. We're buddies, aren't we?"

"Yes."

"I'm listening."

There was an extended pause, then Amieann turned towards Abie and whispered, "There is a ghost in my bedroom that visits me."

Abie gasped and quickly slowed her car down, stopping along the side of the road. "Look at me, please." She paused until Amieann's red eyes met hers. "When I was first hired to teach at Promenade High, I could not find an apartment I wanted to rent, so my father helped me buy and fix up the house we now live in. I inherited a ghost along with the house."

Amieann's eyes opened wide. "You did?" she exclaimed.

"I most certainly did."

"So, you don't think I'm a nut case?"

"You are definitely not a nut case. I know ghosts exist."

"That's a relief," Amieann replied with a slight smile. "So, what did you do about your ghost, or do you still have it?"

"Nope, she is gone. It took a bit of help from others, but we finally got this earthbound spirit to crossover to the other side where it belonged. Take a minute and tell me about your ghost."

"She is dressed like a Native American. At first, I would just see her walk across my room on moonlit nights then disappear, or maybe walk right through the wall. I saw her do that three or four times. Then last night, I woke up and she was standing next to my bed, looking down at me as if she were checking on her child. I didn't scream and wake everyone up. I pulled the blankets over my head and hid under them until morning. She was gone. Can you help me get rid of her?"

"Yes, I definitely can. I gather no one else at home knows about this?"

"No one."

"Good, please keep it that way for now and please stop worrying about this. My ghost was not harmful in any way, and I do not think yours is either. Forget about the horror movies and their mean ghosts. Real ghosts are just stuck here and do not know how to escape to the other side, or Heaven if you like."

"Oh."

"Promise me you will stop worrying about your strange

visitor, and whenever you do think about her, just tell your-self Abie will look after this, okay?"

"I'll try."

"Promise?"

"I promise."

"Good. I am going to contact the others who helped get my ghost to pass over to the other side, and we will work out a plan of action. No more worrying."

Amieann giggled. "Yes, coach."

24

fter Abie dropped Amieann off at her house, and because Rod was on the afternoon shift, Abie drove straight to our house to pick up Normie. Charlotte and Jay-Jay were never in any hurry to see Normie disappear, so while they were entertaining the baby, Abie beckoned us to head for the kitchen after whispering, "We have a problem." Mom stayed with the three kids while Crystal and I pow-wowed with Abie in the kitchen. She quickly explained about Amieann's terrible practice and later confession of a ghost in her bedroom.

After our adventure in Abie's basement with the spirit of Katarina Sosnovich was completed successfully, years earlier, we all agreed that we would forever keep it a secret between us. We did not want the story to spread around Promenade and definitely not around Promenade District High School. In her effort to comfort Amieann, Abie had, without even thinking, broken her promise. She worked herself into a frenzy over this broken promise while she drove to our place and was almost in tears herself as she told us the entire story.

Crystal grabbed Abie in a bear hug and tried to comfort

her when the dam finally shattered and Abie sobbed on her shoulder. This gave me some time to think. I tried to search for all of the possible options to this dilemma, but in the end, there was really only one. Let's face it, none of us would have ignored the desperate pleas of this amazing fourteen-year-old with such an unusual problem that she had absolutely no idea how to deal with. Teachers, by choosing to devote their working years assisting to develop the next generation into upstanding citizens, are sometimes asked for secret advice on personal problems. I always considered it part of the job and did my best to provide appropriate suggestions. I will admit that this was my first, and only, student ghost adventure.

After the flood of tears subsided, Abie composed herself as best she could. I took charge, assuring her that Crystal and I would have done the same thing under the circumstances. I added that as Amieann promised to keep this their secret for now, plus the fact that the Obagato, Radcliff, and Tranter families were quite close, then I was sure that our next secret adventures into the spirit world would still remain a secret from the outside world. Abie agreed that my assessment was correct and assured me she definitely felt better to hear me support her spontaneous reaction to Amieann's unexpected news.

That left us with the necessity of attempting to construct our appropriate plan of action. We needed to let Otto and Marvita know that they would likely be having some unseen visitors in their house. To do that, we would need to introduce them to our spirit guides, and probably their own spirit guides if they were interested in going that far. Getting the three families together without youngsters around was difficult enough, but now that basketball season was upon us, Otto would be on the road a lot. It would be easier to organize a get-together without him, but we certainly were not going to do that behind his back. We had to at least let him know what was going on and why.

Then there was the Amieann problem. How much should we tell a fourteen-year-old about what would be taking place? She might be happy to get rid of her ghost and not really care how we did it. That would be a decision that Otto and Marvita would need to make. All of a sudden, we realized that this challenge could turn out to be even greater than the Katarina Sosnovich adventure. In the end, the three of us decided our best first move was to have Abie phone Otto that evening and advise him that the adults from the three families needed to get together fairly soon to discuss a situation concerning Amieann's welfare. He would also be advised that it was best if he did not question Amieann at all about this situation until we had our three-family get-together and he heard the details of the situation from us.

Abie made her call to Otto and, according to her, it went well. The meeting was set for Sunday afternoon at two at Abie's house. On their drive home after basketball practice on Friday, where Amieann competed like her old self, she told Abie that she would be brother-sitting on Sunday afternoon while the adults were socializing. The two shared a knowing grin and left it at that.

CRYSTAL and I arrived early at Abie and Rod's home, on Sunday afternoon, to pre-plan our strategy as best we could. Rod was playing daddy to Normie, so he was not present in their living room. The Obagatos arrived punctually just before two. Abie prepared finger-snacks and had an assortment of refreshments available, so the get-together began as a social function with casual conversation. I could tell that Otto and Marvita were not at ease through our brief socializing session, so I knew it was time to get down to the business at hand.

"Otto and Marvita," I said, "this is going to sound like a totally off-in-left-field question, I assure you. Do Nigerians talk about spirits or ghosts?"

They both gave me an obviously weird look. "Yes," Otto replied, "Nigerians accept that ghosts and spirits can exist."

"Good. That helps out a lot. Abie, you take over."

All eyes turned to Abie. "Back a few days, did you folks notice that Amieann was not her usual, cheery self?"

"No," Otto replied.

"I did," Marvita said. "A mother knows. She seemed preoccupied about something but would not admit it to me, so I did not hound her about it. Why?"

"She was definitely preoccupied about something. She had a terrible basketball practice on Wednesday. She definitely was not herself. I knew something was bothering her, so on our drive home together I hounded her until she shared her problem with me. She told me she had watched a ghost walk across her bedroom in the night, probably on three occasions, then disappear. Then, in the wee hours of Wednesday morning, she woke up and this ghost was standing next to her bed looking down at her. She did not scream and wake up the house, she just hid under the covers until morning and the ghost was gone.

"Now, I also want to let you know that when my father and I bought this house a number of years ago and fixed it up to what it is today, I also inherited a ghost in the basement along with our purchase. I was in shock and asked John and Crystal for their help in dealing with this unexpected complication in my new home only days after moving in. The process was not simple, but we eventually were able to get the ghost to crossover to the other side, or Heaven if you prefer that term. I am sure we can get Amieann's ghostly visitor to crossover also."

"That's good news," Marvita said. "Is this thing dangerous?"

"Only in the movies. Most real ghosts are simply spirits that for some reason did not manage to make the transition to the other side at the time of the death of the body they had resided in. Our challenge will be to figure out why Amieann's ghost is still here and how to help her cross over. Amieann did say she appeared to be a Native American in appearance."

"Okay, what do we do now?" Otto asked.

"Are you familiar with the term Spirit Guide?" I asked.

"I have heard the term but must admit I do not know much about it."

"We all have a Spirit Guide dedicated to assisting us along our journey during our current lifetime. We may also have other guides who assist us with more unique problems when they crop up. Crystal and I talk with our spirit guides often. Would you like to meet them?"

Marvita chocked. "Are you serious?"

"I would not joke about this, believe me. It is our spirit guides that will hopefully assist Amieann's ghost to crossover, just like they did with Abie's stranded basement spirit years ago. They are here with us now, I'm pretty sure, but they stay invisible unless invited to appear. I will ask my Spirit Guide to appear if you are ready to witness this. He is really friendly."

Marvita grinned. "This is unbelievable, but go ahead and make it believable. I'm ready to be convinced."

"Tom, please show yourself to us." Tom commenced to slowly materialize beside me.

"Hello, Otto and Marvita. It is nice to finally meet you face to face, so to speak," Tom said with a grin.

Marvita just stared for a few seconds. "Hello, Tom. I guess you just made the unbelievable believable."

"I'm sure it will take you a little while to get used to this new reality, but you will," Tom assured her. "Would you like to also meet Crystal's Spirit Guide? Because Abie's earthbound spirit had lived in the body of a female and was deathly afraid of men, it was Crystal's Spirit Guide who was primarily responsible for setting up the process for this spirit to crossover. Since Amieann's ghost apparently was a female, Courtney will likely be of great assistance in arranging for this spirit to crossover also. Would you like to meet Courtney?"

"Why not," Otto declared.

"Courtney, please show yourself to all of us," Crystal said.

Courtney slowly materialized in front of Crystal. "Hi, everyone. Thanks for the invitation. Those goodies look delicious. Too bad I cannot eat any."

We all got a good chuckle out of Courtney's delightful attitude, and I noticed that Otto and Marvita showed signs of relaxing. "That brings us to a question I need to ask. There is definitely no pressure on you to do so, Otto and Marvita, but now that you know Spirit Guides really do exist, would you like to meet your Spirit Guides?"

The shock of the unanticipated question was registered on both faces. They looked at each other and shrugged their shoulders, obviously uncertain what they should do. I took that as a clue. "What do you say we keep that in abeyance for a while and just take one small step for now? I suspect Courtney and Tom know your Spirit Guides by name and even hang around with them when we get together in one place like this. Is that correct, Courtney?"

"You know it is."

"I know, but Otto and Marvita did not know. If you two would like to know the names of your Spirit Guides, you must actually request that they be revealed by Courtney or Tom. The advantage of knowing their names is that if sometime in the future when you are alone and relaxed, you could ask them to appear for you just like we requested Tom and Courtney to appear here today. Again, there is no pressure on you to do this, so the decision is entirely yours."

Marvita and Otto looked at each other and both nodded. "Please reveal the name of my Spirit Guide," Marvita said.

"Your Spirit Guide is called Lois," Courtney replied. "By the way, she is very nice."

"Thank you, Courtney. Okay, Otto, your turn."

"Please reveal the name of my Spirit Guide," Otto said.

"Your Spirit Guide is called David. He is pretty nice, too," Tom responded.

"Thank you. Now I have a question for you, Tom. How come both of our Spirit Guides have common American names instead of Nigerian names from back where we were born?"

"All of you in the room, your relatives, all of your and their Spirit Guides, plus many other souls, are part of the same soul group. Before a round of incarnations, our group gets together and decides where some of us will incarnate, at least partially based on the needs of group members' souls to progress. I know this is confusing, but all souls were created at the same time by God, or the Universe if you prefer. Souls incarnate to progress to their original God-like state. Probably all of us have sinned or acted poorly towards others in previous incarnations, so we have lessons to learn. The lessons we need to learn are a main factor in determining the location and the body we choose to incarnate in, or alternately not incarnate this round but act as a spirit guide for others instead, like me. Back to your question, Otto, the plan for your soul and Marvita's this incarnation was to be here in America but your early years in Nigeria allowed you to learn some needed lessons before coming here. Your Spirit Guides knew you would be here before you learned they existed, so they chose their names accordingly. Hopefully that makes some sense."

"That is a heck of a lot to grasp at one time, but I certainly understand the point about the names of our Spirit Guides," Otto said.

"That leaves you lots of things you can ask David when you begin talking with him," Tom added.

"That is true. Changing topics, what are we going to do about Amieann's ghost?" Otto asked.

"If you will grant me permission to invisibly visit your home," Courtney said, "I will do so soon and see if I can make contact with Amieann's ghost."

"Have you not already been in our home when Crystal visits with us?" Otto asked.

"Good question," Courtney responded. "Yes, I have been there before with Crystal, but while there I remain with Crystal and do not snoop all around your house. Amieann's ghost did not make an appearance when we were all together. I now require your permission to snoop around your entire house and see what I discover."

"I see. I now grant you permission to visit and snoop around our home as often as required to assist our ghost to move on to the other side where it belongs," Otto stated.

25

Courtney waited until the teachers and students were off to school on Monday morning before heading over to the Obagato home to pursue Amieann's ghost. She noticed Marvita sitting in the living room reading a book and decided it was appropriate for her to advise the homeowner of her presence. Once again, I am creating conversations based on the information Courtney relayed to Crystal and me later on that day.

"Marvita, it is Courtney," she said as she began to materialize across the room.

Marvita immediately jumped before her mind processed what was taking place. "Good morning, Courtney. I wondered if you would visit with us this morning."

"Good morning. When I spotted you here, I thought I should alert you of my presence in case you heard conversations in your house and wondered what was going on."

"Thank you. Now that I know, it will not bother me."

"Wonderful. I shall be off to see what I can find."

Courtney floated up the stairs and noticed that all of the bedroom doors were open. The first door on the right was obviously Marvita and Otto's room. The first door on the left, with bunk beds, was obviously Derrick and Dwight's room. She stopped at the next door on the left and looked inside. Over near the rear corner, between a dresser and a window, stood the figure of a Native American woman. "Hello there," she called out.

The ghost jumped. "Hello."

"Is it okay if I come in?"

"Okay. I talk little English."

Courtney walked over closer to the woman. "My name is Courtney."

"Me, Rainbow."

"You live here?"

"Yes. Home not same, now."

"You live here alone?"

"No, husband white man."

"What is your husband's name?"

"Shane O'Reilly."

"Is Shane here now?"

"No. No come back yet."

"Where did he go?"

"Hunting."

"You said the house was not the same now. How do you remember it?"

"Log cabin. Only open room and bedroom."

"Tell me about the last time you saw your log cabin, please."

"Woke up in night. Cracking noise somewhere and smoke in bedroom. Opened door and fire all over big room."

"Thank you for the information, Rainbow. Is it okay if I visit you again?"

"Yes. Nobody here talk to me."

"Bye." Courtney turned and slowly walked to the door, waving before she disappeared around the corner. She floated down to the living room and was happy to find Marvita still in her chair. "I'm back, Marvita."

Marvita looked up from her book. "Hi. How did you make out?"

"Pretty good, I think. We had a short chat. Her name is Rainbow. She was married to a Shane O'Reilly so she may have been called Rainbow O'Reilly. They lived in a log cabin way back, apparently on this land. There was a fire, and she was apparently caught in it. I did not push for details."

"I can certainly see why. That must have been terrible."

"Definitely. Did you use a local lawyer to close your purchase of this property?"

"Yes. He is in Promenade."

"Good. He should have checked the land registry records to make sure the title to this property was free and clear. Could you please contact him and ask if the name Shane O'Reilly showed up in the records and let Crystal know what you find out. It is always possible that Rainbow's cabin was not actually on this property, but only nearby."

"I will do that right now. By the way, how do you know so much about land registry records?"

"I was a lawyer in my most recent incarnation. I told Rainbow I would come back and visit so I will return soon, I hope," Courtney said and disappeared.

Courtney brought Crystal and me up to date on her visit to the Obagato house when she invisibly popped into the back seat of my car as we drove home from school. Abie and Amieann had a basketball practice, so we were able to share our update with Abie in the kitchen while Mom and our kids entertained Normie in the living room. During that conversation we agreed that we needed to advise Otto and Marvita of our wishes that this ghostly adventure we were embarking on needed to be kept a secret amongst the three families. Marvita assured us later that they had no intention of telling anyone about their ghost problem or sharing any details with Amieann. After the younger ones were in bed in both houses, Marvita called Crystal with the information on the earlier owners of the Obagato property.

Shane O'Reilly owned the property and constructed a cabin on it back in the late eighteen hundreds. About ten years later, he stopped paying the property taxes on the property. When a township employee went out to visit him, all he found was the remnants of the long-burnt-down cabin. The township apparently never heard anything from Shane O'Reilly from that point on. Years later, the Township seized the property for unpaid back taxes and owned the vacant property for many decades. As the town began to grow and expand its boundaries, the township decided to sell the property at market value. A local family purchased it and constructed a new house there. Two decades later this family sold the property to Otto and Marvita. Courtney was present when Crystal updated my parents and me after Marvita's telephone call.

Courtney returned to the Obagato home on Tuesday morning and located Marvita reading a book in the same chair as the day before. "Good morning, Marvita," she called out as she materialized.

"Good morning, Courtney. To be honest, I have been expecting you."

"I'm not surprised. Thank you for gathering the information on the previous owners of your property. It will help me with my chore to try and convince Rainbow to crossover to the other side. I know we did not give you the details concerning how we dealt with Abie's basement spirit. The truth is that I did the groundwork, but we were able to persuade the spirit's brother to visit her and hopefully convince her to crossover, which he succeeded in doing, so I really have no first-hand experience doing this."

"I am sure you can handle it."

"That is what they keep telling me. "I'm off. I'll let you know how it goes."

Courtney located Rainbow standing in the same spot in Amieann's bedroom as she did the previous day. "Hi, Rainbow," she called out as she walked towards her.

"Hi, Courtney."

That was all Rainbow said. She just stood there looking at Courtney. "Did Shane come home yet?" Courtney asked for openers.

"Not yet. Sometimes he gone long time."

"I know. I am sorry to have to tell you that Shane will not be coming back this time."

Rainbow gave her a sad look. "Why Shane not come back?"

"I want you to think back to that night you woke up to the crackling sound and smoke in your bedroom. Then you opened the door and saw the fire all around the big room."

"I no like think about that."

"I understand. What did you do after you saw all of the fire in the big room?"

"Closed door and ran to window."

"Then what did you do?"

"Break glass with Shane's boot."

"Did you climb out the window?"

Rainbow paused in contemplation. "I not remember."

"You do not remember being outside the cabin and running away from the fire?"

"No."

"Do you understand what that means?"

"No."

"Rainbow did not get out the window. She died in the cabin fire."

"No. Rainbow here."

"Did you eat breakfast this morning?"

"No."

"Did you sleep in your bed last night?"

"No. Girl in bed."

"Did you eat dinner last night?"

"No."

"Rainbow, listen to me carefully. You and I do not have bodies like the girl in the bed. We are both spirits. We are no longer human beings. Can you walk through walls? I can."

"Yes."

"Human's cannot walk through walls. Come. Let's you and I walk outside, right through this wall, together, okay?" Courtney walked over to the wall on the other side of the window and looked back. "Come," she said again and walked through the wall. Rainbow followed behind her within seconds. "See? We are no longer humans," she said when they were both in the backyard.

"I not understand."

"Let me try and explain. All humans have souls and spirit in their bodies. When their bodies die, their souls and spirits leave the bodies and go to visit the Gods in the sky. That is what usually happens, but sometimes, as in your case, if a body dies totally unexpectedly, the soul and spirit do not go to the sky with the Gods. These spirits remain here where the body died and do not know what to do or where to go, like you."

"And like you?"

"Actually, no. I have, what we call, crossed over to the other side, which allows me to travel back and forth to the Gods and back here on land whenever I wish. You are stuck here right now, or what we call earthbound. But that is only temporary. I hope to show you how to crossover like I did and there is a big bonus in doing that because you will be able to see Shane and your parents again, probably."

"I like that. Why you say probably?"

THE DOOR TO FOREVER

"I know how to help spirits cross over, but I have never done it before. I should not have told you probably because I am pretty sure you and I can do this. I gather you do want to crossover?"

"Oh yes. I want be with Shane and parents again."

"Good. Shall we try this?"

"Yes."

"Have you ever noticed a patch of yellow like a very small sun but not up in the sky? It is down here close to the land. For some reason I do not understand myself, I am not able to see this yellow area because I am not earthbound."

"I see it often, but it reminds me of fire so I stay away from it."

"Can you see it now?"

"Yes, out in front of us."

"Please listen carefully to me. This yellow patch is a doorway to the Gods and your family. There is no reason to be afraid of it. When you get really close to it, you will see at least some of your relatives waiting to welcome you to the other side. For some reason I cannot really explain, they are unable to come and get you. You need to go to them, and when you go through this yellow patch, which is really a door, you will no longer be stuck here alone. Okay?"

Rainbow did not answer.

"Try not to be afraid. I promise you that you will be very happy when you go through the yellow doorway, okay? Remember, when you get up close you will see some relatives beckoning to you. If you do not see your relatives you do not need to go through the door, okay? I will walk along with you if you like, but I will not be able to see the yellow door or your relatives. I have already been welcomed by my relatives in the past."

"Okay. Please walk with me."

"I will. Come." Courtney started walking forward and

Rainbow followed close behind her. "Remember that I cannot see the door, so you need to guide me in the correct direction."

"Go little to your right."

"Okay. Come up beside me." Courtney waited for Rainbow to catch up and take a small lead.

They walked in silence for a short while and then Rainbow screeched, "Shane, Shane, I am coming to you! Thank you, Courtney," she called out before she disappeared.

Courtney sighed. "Thank you, my Father in Heaven. I could not have done this without you."

26

The Obagato family quickly became good friends with the Radcliffs and us Tranters. Derrick Obagato was a year older than Charlotte, and Dwight was a year older than Jay-Jay. They went to different elementary schools so when they had the opportunity to get to see each other the four of them loved playing together, in our old barn and backfield, as well as in the bush and around the pond at the new home of the Obagatos.

Amieann was the star of the girls' basketball team throughout her high school days. The team finished first in our local league every year and advanced to the regional finals the third year, losing in the semi-finals by five points. In Amieann's senior year the team won the regionals but was not competitive against the state's other champions. Amieann earned a full-ride basketball scholarship to the Ivy League University that Otto scouted for. She studied Human Kinetics and received her teaching credentials as a Physical Education teacher, but never managed to put them to use. She happened to fall in love with the star of the University's men's basketball team. He was drafted by an NBA team and experienced a rather successful, fifteen-year professional career with three different teams in three divergent cities around the country. By the time he retired, Amieann was spending much of her time corralling her three active youngsters. She returned to visit us folks in the Promenade-Mantle area when she could but never resided here again.

This chapter of my story, and our lives, is going to seem like a stewpot of information. The kid years, when the children of the three families were growing up, were amazing times that I would not have missed, believe me, but that period did not include the same type of excitement generated by our ghost-hunting escapades. I will give you a little snippet on each of the activities of the next generation.

Like Crystal, Abie decided to have a second child a year and a half after Normie was born. Also, like Crystal, she decided to resign her teaching position and stay home with her youngsters until they started school. We did not have any ex-staff members waiting in the wings to replace her, so we needed to hire from outside of our school area. We were fortunate to hire a senior teacher out of Lexington who was eager to escape the bigger city and return to a rural area similar to where he was raised. Stuart and Rachael Dobbs were nice folks and fit into our school and rural community quite well. They had two daughters attending college and no younger children at home, so they did not spend a lot of personal time with us Tranters, Radcliffs, and Obagatos, where our youngsters ruled our free time.

Angelique Margarete Radcliff was born in June. She was quickly christened Angel and she truly was an Angel. It was impossible not to spoil her, trust me. As the youngest of the Tranter, Radcliff, and Obagato clans, she was amply spoiled by all of us. Fortunately, Abie made sure that it did not get carried away as Angel grew up and she eventually turned into an amazing young lady. More about that later.

When Angel was due to start kindergarten in the fall, Abie was keen to get back into teaching at Promenade District High School. Remember Nancy Rutledge? You have read this before, but a little refresher is likely advisable. Nancy was the English teacher I replaced at Promenade High when she requested her pregnancy leave, then later resigned her position, erasing my status as a temporary teacher. When Crystal was pregnant, Nancy returned to Promenade High as her replacement and stayed on when Crystal resigned her position. Nancy, Abie, and Crystal all taught together, although not necessarily all at the same time when one was home raising their offspring. The three ladies got along marvelously and were great friends.

When Nancy's husband was contemplating retirement, Nancy approached Abie as to whether she wished to return to teaching when Angel was ready to start school. Abie said yes, so Nancy advised her that she and her husband would synchronize their retirement plans with Abie's availability to return to teaching fulltime so she could rejoin us at Promenade District High School.

It may sound to readers that the way the resignations and convenient rehirings took place at Promenade High is impossible to be real, but it isn't. All three ladies were fabulous English teachers, and there was no way the principal and I, as the Head of the English Department, were going to pass them up and gamble on an outsider. When you have a good thing going for you, don't rock the boat, and we didn't.

Back to the offspring. Our Charlotte took after her mother. She had little interest in sports but was nuts about reading and acting, as was her mother. Charlotte tried out for and received parts in all of the school plays, including the musicals that involved singing. I hope she is not hurt when she reads this, but she was a fabulous actress and a so-so singer. Actually, she knew that herself and often admitted it to us. She went on to study English and Theatre Arts in University and became a teacher in both of those subjects. Unfortunately, not at Promenade High.

Jay-Jay loved to play baseball but was not especially gifted at it. His main interest was in scientific research, more specifically Astrophysics. He read everything he could get his hands or eyes on, received a PhD in Astrophysics and was hired by NASA. More about our delightful offspring later, but in this chapter, I want to include the activities and successes of the Radcliff and Obagato children as well.

Derrick Obagato was an excellent basketball player, like his father. Unfortunately, he was hampered by genetics. Marvita Obagato was over a foot shorter than Otto and Derrick inherited her height genes. Derrick was a star on our high school basketball team, but the scouts, including his father, knew he would never receive a college scholarship. He knew it also. He decided to study Medicine and became a Doctor. Although he was born in the United States, he maintained a keen interest in his parents' homeland, Nigeria. Derrick decided he would devote his life to providing health services to the needy in Nigeria and neighboring African countries. He made sure he returned home at least once a year to visit with us in the Promenade-Mantle communities, and it was wonderful as well as heartbreaking to listen to him share some of his experiences as a volunteer Doctor in Africa.

Dwight Obagato was a clone of his father. He had the height and talent to become a star and did. He led the Promenade District High School boys' basketball teams to many league and regional championships, but our little town still could not capture a state championship. He received a full-ride, basketball scholarship to the same Ivey League University as Amieann had and the same university that Otto scouted for. Dwight was a good university basketball player but not a star and was never drafted by any of the NBA teams.

He acquired a degree in Physical Education as well as his teaching papers. It was not his first stop, just like me, but Dwight eventually joined our teaching staff and, like me, returned to his alma mater to teach.

Boy, we at Promenade District High School had certainly come a long way! We had two graduates, Dwight and Amieann Obagato, who graduated from Promenade High and received full-ride, university basketball scholarships. Also, we had two teachers, Dwight and Abie, coaching our basketball teams, who had received full-ride, university basketball scholarships. I am sure you do not remember way back to Abie's original hiring at Promenade High that the girls' basketball coach was a teacher on staff with only high school basketball-playing experience. We had definitely come a long way. Guess what? We are not done yet.

I left the youngest kids to the last, Abie and Rod's adorable ones, as they were the youngsters of that generation. Normie was an exceptional athlete, which shouldn't be a big surprise with his mother being a former basketball star and Abie's father being a noted, college football lineman. He was very good at all sports, participated in many of them, but his heart was in baseball. He pulled in a full-ride, baseball scholarship at the college his mother and grandfather stared for. He was also drafted by a major league baseball team, in the second round. He chose to go to college, for starters, and excelled so outstandingly there that the major league baseball team offered him a fat contract to turn pro after two years. He could not turn it down. He worked his way up quickly through their minor pro teams and made his major league debut in September of his third professional season. The next year he was installed as their starting center fielder and went on to experience a very successful, fifteen-year major league career.

Angelique, or Angel as we all called her, also inherited the athletic genes from her mother's side. She was an excellent, all-round athlete and received a partial college scholarship in track and field. As good as she was in numerous sports, her heart belonged to her father's dedicated career as a police officer. She studied Criminology and, with her Master's Degree in Criminology, pursued a very successful career with the FBI, investigating activities that she was forbidden to even talk about to outsiders.

27

With the histories out of the way, I need to take you back to Charlotte and Jay-Jay. Remember back a number of chapters? Probably not. I mentioned that after Charlotte started kindergarten, leaving Jay-Jay home alone all day for a year, Crystal and Mom suspected he enjoyed an invisible playmate. Jay-Jay told them his name was Robbie. From that point on, Crystal and Mom often were certain that Robbie made regular visits to Jay-Jay, but the ladies never questioned him about Robbie and Jay-Jay never offered us any information on his own accord.

A decade and a half later, when Charlotte went off to University, Jay-Jay was once again left as the only child at home. Mom, Dad, Crystal, and I often consulted our Spirit Guides throughout the years, but just like Jay-Jay kept quiet about Robbie, we never mentioned to him about our Spirit Guides either. I cannot give you a definitive reason for this other than that the ideal opportunity never seemed to present itself for us to do so. The four of us often chatted, when he wasn't around, about starting a conversation with Jay-Jay concerning invisible friends and Spirit Guides. We agreed that we should breach the topic whenever the opportunity finally presented itself. One Sunday afternoon in the fall, we were sitting around the living room during a stormy, rainy day and Crystal figured there was no better time than the present to flip that long-unturned page.

"Jay, do you remember back when you were four you told Grandma and me you enjoyed playing with Robbie?"

Jay cocked his head and was momentarily silent. "Did I say that?"

"Yes, you did," Grandma added.

"Oh," Jay-Jay said softly and chewed on his lip.

"It's okay, Honey," Crystal said. "Mom, Dad, Grandma, and Grandpa all have invisible friends that we call Spirit Guides."

"Oh!" Jay-Jay blurted out, followed by a wide grin. "Why didn't you ever tell me about that before?"

"Good question," Crystal responded. "I guess the best reason I can give you was that we were never sure if you were ready to talk to us about this rather unusual subject. Would you like to meet our Spirit Guides?"

"Oh yes."

Crystal asked Courtney to show herself, and then I asked Tom to appear as well. Grandma proceeded to invite in Malory to join us, followed by Grandpa asking Alexander to join the party. The grin on Jay-Jay's face was priceless and none of us had a camera handy. This was still back before cellphones.

After the pop-ins and introductions were completed, Jay-Jay took over. "Robbie, please show yourself to us." Robbie materialized next to Jay-Jay.

"Boy, I am sure glad that you folks finally got that over with," Robbie teased. "Do you know how long we guides have been waiting for this day to arrive?"

Everyone laughed. "I thought time stood still on your side," Crystal replied.

"It does," Robbie said, "and it's a good thing for that or we would have been throwing snowballs at you folks years ago."

Everyone enjoyed another good laugh. "Ya, sure you would," Crystal countered. The ten of us proceeded to enjoy a marvelous, lengthy, unreserved conversation about Spirit Guides and our soul group. I will skip most of it but not this.

"Jay, does Charlotte know anything about any of this?" Crystal asked.

"Yes, pretty much," Jay-Jay replied. "When I was around ten or so, I asked her whether she was ever visited by any strange children when she could not really explain where they suddenly came from or disappeared to. She gave me an *are you crazy look,* so I told her about Robbie's visits. She insisted that I was just making it all up at first, so I offered to ask Robbie to appear so she could meet him. She thought about that for a minute or two, probably still not believing me, so she dared me to have him appear. Her mistake. I invited Robbie to visit with us, and he began to materialize somewhat behind and off to the side of me so he did not frighten her too much. She turned as white as a sheet. You'd think she saw a ghost or something."

We all roared at that one. "Don't stop now," Crystal pleaded.

"I won't. Robbie and I gave her a minute to settle her heartbeat back down. 'He talks too,' I added. 'Robbie, say hello to my white-as-a-sheet sister.'

"'Hello, Charlotte. I am happy to finally get a chance to meet you.'

"'Finally? What do you mean?'

"'I am what is called a Spirit Guide, more specifically Jay's Spirit Guide. As his Spirit Guide, I hang around him most of the time, so I have seen you often for years.'

"'Oh. Even in my bedroom or the bathtub?'

"'No, no. We are not snoops. Our function is to guide you and when possible protect you when you are in danger.'

"'Oh. You protect me too?'

"'Sort of, when you are with Jay.'

"'And when I am alone?'

"'Your Spirit Guide does that.'

"'Oh, why haven't I met her or him?'

"'She has always been around you since you were born, but because you did not know she existed, she simply did her job in silence.'

"'Oh. Is she here now?'

"'Of course. Her name is Heather. Would you finally like to meet her?'

"Charlotte hesitated, obviously uncertain. 'Don't be a chicken,' I teased her.

"'Shut up! I am not a chicken.'

"'You could have fooled me,' I shot back.

"Robbie and I waited in silence as she debated with herself whether this was really such a good idea or not. 'Okay,' she said, barely above a whisper. 'I'll meet her.'

"'You need to actually invite her,' Robbie said. 'Say, "Heather, please let me see you."'

"'There was another pause and then she said, "Heather, please let me see you." Heather then materialized over beside Robbie and me. Charlotte just stared at her for a little while.

"'Thank you for allowing me to become visible to you,' Heather started off for openers. Once Charlotte relaxed sufficiently, she and Heather had a great time getting acquainted. Robbie and I just hung around and listened to them jibber back and forth. Charlotte later thanked me for opening this whole new door for her. Heather, Robbie, Charlotte and I enjoyed numerous get-togethers over the years from that point on."

28

I t was a four-hour drive to Charlotte's university, so we had not seen her since the first term started in September. The students there, and in our school district as well, enjoyed a one-week break on Thanksgiving week. Saturday morning Crystal and I set out to meet Charlotte, along with her university roommate and girlfriend, for lunch and then haul them both back to our farm for the week.

Charlotte's roommate, Antonia Gonzales, usually called Toni, was from Puerto Rico and it was too expensive for her to fly home for a week on the break. This was a common problem for foreign students and others a long way from home, so many universities and colleges allowed these students to remain in the residences over the breaks, especially Thanksgiving and Christmas. Charlotte felt sorry for Toni on this accord and asked us if she could bring her new friend home with her. Of course we said yes.

Toni was a beautiful, well mannered, shy young lady and we were delighted to enjoy her company for the week. She was Hispanic and possessed a full head of wavy-curly, jet black hair which perfectly suited her olive skin color and brown eyes. She had an infectious smile and a slim figure, as did many healthy eighteen-year-olds. To be perfectly honest, she was a knockout. Jay-Jay could not keep his eyes off of her and developed an instant crush on her. It took a few days, but we soon discovered that she quickly felt the same way towards him. More about that shortly.

On the drive back to the farm Charlotte and Toni filled Crystal and me in on many of the goings-on at their university. Mom had a scrumptious dinner waiting for all of us on our arrival back home, and after the four ladies took care of the leftovers and dishes, we all settled into the living room and chatted away for hours. Close to bedtime, Toni asked if she could hop into the shower. Charlotte showed her where everything was located and then rejoined us in the living room. Jay-Jay seized the opportunity.

"Listen, sis, a few weeks back everyone confided in me that they all had Spirit Guides like we do and they conversed with them from time to time. We all invited in our Spirit Guides, and the ten of us had a wonderful gab session. Mom asked, so I told them about you and Heather and we eagerly looked forward to having you home for the week so you and Heather could join our party. Toni is a marvelous young lady, but unfortunately she throws a wrench into our original plan."

Charlotte gave us a mischievous grin. "No, she doesn't. Toni and I, along with our Spirit Guides, have lots of chats."

"Fantastic. How did you know she knew anything about Spirit Guides?"

"One day when Toni was at a late class, I was chatting with Heather and did not hear Toni enter our dorm room. She asked me why I was talking to myself. I got flustered and turned beet red I'm sure. I made up something to the effect that it was just a bad habit of mine, but she didn't buy it. I guess she heard more than I thought she heard. She asked me if I was talking to my Spirit Guide and added that she talks to her Spirit Guide all the time. I was certainly relieved to hear that so we both invited our guides to show themselves to us and we had the first of many group discussions."

"That is super news," Crystal said. "Do you think she and her Spirit Guide would like to join the twelve of us in a group chat?"

"I'm sure of it. It is way too late now to get into that, but I will share the news with Toni tonight when we're alone, and I am positive we can assemble a group of fourteen one day before we return to school. This sounds very exciting to me, and I had no idea that the rest of you were talking to your Spirit Guides."

Everybody enjoyed sleeping in late on Sunday morning. Well, all except Mom. I guess you can never really change a farm wife. I woke up to the mouth-watering aroma of home-made buns, and pretty quickly, our group of seven was assembled around the big dining room table. Mom had the eggs and bacon all ready to slip into the frying pan when the parade of footsteps made its way down the stairs. Crystal and Toni helped Mom clean up the dishes while Charlotte called some of her close friends to chat and make plans to get together sometime throughout their break from classes.

After a late lunch, the sun had plenty of time to warm things up outside. Charlotte asked Toni if she would like to take a walk around the farm, and she eagerly accepted. Jay-Jay gave his sister the sad-puppy-dog look, and she invited him to join them if he wanted to. Of course he did. Crystal and Mom worked on preparing a big Sunday dinner for the gang, and it was eagerly devoured by all. After the kitchen cleanup, we were contentedly lounging in the living room when Charlotte abruptly changed the topic of conversation.

"I mentioned to Toni last night that, while she was enjoying her shower, all of you admitted you have Spirit Guides that you are aware of and communicate with. She previously was only aware that I knew about Jay's and my Spirit Guides, so this revelation took her quite by surprise when she heard it. I also told her that you had group discussions with all of your guides just like she and I do back in our dorm room. I then asked if she was interested in joining in with our family's group discussion and she thought it was a wonderful idea. Does anyone object to us initiating a group discussion right now?"

Everyone was eager to proceed. Crystal and I invited Courtney and Tom to make an appearance, then Mom and Dad invited Malory and Alexander to join us. Toni flashed a wide, adorable grin at that point. Jay-Jay was next, and Robbie made his presence known, immediately followed by Charlotte inviting Heather to materialize as well. Toni quickly invited her guide, Consuelo, to round out our group of fourteen.

"Consuelo," Toni said, "it's apparent that the Tranters know way more about what is going on here than I do. Do you know all of these spirit guides?"

"Yes."

"How come?"

"All fourteen of us here are part of the same soul group. Our souls have known each other for many thousands of years. The fourteen of us, as well as many, many others, incarnate together from time to time to assist each other's spiritual development. All of us are not always together, and when some of us are together we are usually in different positions. That is not a great explanation, I'm sure. Let me give you an example. In a future round of incarnations, I could be a man and Tom could be my wife. You might be my son and Charlotte might be my Spirit Guide. The other ten here might not even be incarnated at that time. The purpose of souls incarnating into human bodies is education or development of our souls. Our souls need to work on certain experiences from our past where we were lacking in some way, and other souls will incarnate with us to assist us in our development that time around. Using a totally fictitious example, you may have been the mother of ten children five hundred years ago and were so overwhelmed with this responsibility that you could not stand it anymore, so you ran away and joined the circus. That would leave your soul lacking in the mothering qualities so you might be here now to practice being a better mother than your past record shows. Remember, I just made that up, but do you get the idea?"

"I think so. In that case, I would need to improve the way I treat and care for children. Is that what they call bad karma?"

"Precisely."

"Okay, so why am I here now?"

"You won't like the answer. I can't tell you."

"Then how am I supposed to advance my soul if I don't know what I need to work on?"

"You, Toni the human, do not know why you are here, but your soul does know. If something doesn't feel right in your heart or conscience, then that is often a quality you need to work on this time around. Be kind. Be helpful. Do not be mean or selfish. Sincere kindness is the fastest road to erasing your past transgressions. Make sense?"

"Absolutely. Can I go on?"

"Of course. I'm not going anyplace. You're stuck with me whether you like it or not."

"I'll remember that. Okay, three months ago I did not know the Tranters existed. The university placed Charlotte and I in the same dorm room, and now here I am, the guest of this wonderful family. Was that just luck or part of my soul's plan?"

"Part of your soul's plan."

"So, I was destined to meet and be closely connected to them?"

"Yes."

"Is there more to it than that?"

"If you make it so."

"That's not a lot of help."

"Part of your challenge is to figure things out."

"Thanks a bundle. Will Charlotte and I be life-long friends?"

"If you and Charlotte want it to be that way."

"Could there be other reasons?"

"If you want it that way?"

"How about some examples here, even if they are fictitious? That would be a big help."

"That's fair. Let's see. If you were to study nursing or home care services, then you might end up looking after Charlotte's grandparents in their old age. If you became a person who cleaned other people's houses, then you might end up practicing your talents in this very house. Let's go for one more. Maybe Charlotte brought you here to meet Jay-Jay so you two could one day become man and wife."

"Yes! That's it," Jay-Jay declared in a loud voice. Everyone had a hardy laugh, but Toni and Jay-Jay both turned scarlet. The room fell silent for maybe thirty seconds, but Jay was not done. "Consuelo, may I ask you some questions?"

"Certainly."

"I know you were just giving Toni some hypothetical reasons why she suddenly became aware of her connections to us Tranters, but since you mentioned me, I would appreciate more background information if you are allowed to reveal it. Have Toni and I enjoyed previous lifetimes together, and if so, how many?"

"Five."

"Super. Were we ever husband and wife in any of them?"

"Yes. You were a couple back in Rome many hundreds of years ago, but you were the female in that life."

"Oh. Okay, how were we associated in the other four?"

"You were Toni's father once. You were two brothers another time. She was your mother way, way back, and you were her Spirit Guide once when she was female."

"So, if we married in this lifetime with me as a male, then it would be a new experience for our souls, right?"

"That is correct."

"Was that in our souls' plans for this lifetime?"

Consuelo hesitated for a few seconds. "Let me just say that is something you two will need to figure out for yourselves."

"I am definitely going to work on that," Jay-Jay commented, giving Toni a noticeable wink that caused her to blush once more.

29

The Tranter residents, except my dad who was off to work and my mom who always got up with him, enjoyed the beginning of their week off by lazily sneaking some extra pillow time on Monday morning. After a leisurely breakfast, Charlotte and Toni prepared to head out for a morning walk. "You can come along with us if you like, Casanova," Charlotte teased her brother.

"I would love to if it is okay with Toni," he sheepishly replied.

Toni tried hard not to grin but failed miserably. "I am trained in self-defense, so I will be quite safe." Everyone enjoyed a good laugh and the threesome headed towards the back door.

Both Charlotte and Jay-Jay possessed driver's licenses, so after lunch, Charlotte was off in Crystal's car to Promenade to visit with one of her closest friends from high school, who was also in town only for the week. She invited Toni to come along, but Toni politely declined the kind offer, insisting she and her girlfriend did not need her hanging around while they caught up on their adventures at university. Toni added she should do some work on her biology project.

Charlotte could not have made it out the driveway and onto the concession road before Jay-Jay jumped into action. "It is a beautiful afternoon out there. How about you and I going out for another walk and grabbing some rays? We can do homework on rainy days and evenings."

Toni hesitated a few seconds. "Good plan. Let's enjoy the warm weather while it lasts."

The two of them disappeared out the back door within a minute or so. Crystal and I figured we might as well seize the opportunity to mark some essays we brought home for our vacation week. Over two hours later, we realized the young duo had not yet returned from their walk. We checked out the back window, and they were nowhere in sight. "That's interesting," I commented.

"Maybe they walked along the concession road a ways," Crystal speculated. It was not much later when Toni and Jay walked into the living room holding hands. Déjà vu struck me like lightning. I remembered, as if it were yesterday, when some twenty plus years ago Crystal and I stunned my parents when we walked in holding hands for the first time and I announced that we were now boyfriend and girlfriend.

"Toni and I had a nice long conversation concerning whether our souls could really have actually planned for us to be here together at this time in order to get to know each other better and then maybe someday down the road even get married," Jay said with a wide grin. "We agreed we should spend as much time together as we can when we have an opportunity to do so and hopefully comprehend our compatibility."

Crystal and I glanced at each other and grinned. I am sure she also remembered that day two-plus decades ago when we walked in, hand in hand, to surprise my parents. "I think that is a marvelous plan," Crystal stated.

Thanksgiving week sped by way too fast, as usual. It was super having Charlotte and Toni home with us for the week. Jay-Jay's and Toni's plan to get to know each other seemed to go well. They held hands at times, stretched an arm around the other on occasions, joked, teased each other, and worked on their school projects side by side at the dining room table. Another plus going for them was that they both had scientific minds. Jay was already talking about researching the world of astrophysics, and Toni was striving for a career in biological research.

Jay would place a quick kiss on Toni's cheek now and then, but we never witnessed any passionate embraces. They enjoyed numerous walks together, sometimes with Charlotte tagging along when available. We also suspected they discovered the advantages of the hayloft in the old barn that Crystal and I patronized so passionately two-plus decades earlier. Toni arrived back inside one afternoon following a long walk, and whatever else might have taken place, with a couple of small pieces of straw stuck in her adorable head of wavy-curly, black hair. Only one place around where that could happen.

Saturday evening, with over-stuffed stomachs from the scrumptious, going-away dinner prepared by Mom and Crystal, we were all assembled in the living room for our last group-of-seven get-together for who knew how long. Everyone's assurances that it had been a monumental delight having her join us for the week had me fearing that Toni's blushing complexion would become permanent. She heartily thanked us for one of the most memorable weeks of her life.

The always surprising and often conniving Jay-Jay jumped in. "I would like to drive down and visit Charlotte and Toni some weekends if I can use your car, Mom. I hope to leave after school on Fridays and return Sunday evening. Would that be okay with you guys?"

"Where would you stay?"

"He can actually stay in our dorm room with us," Charlotte advised. "Many students have overnight company, so this is nothing unusual. We need to advise the office staff at the dorm as to who our overnight company is and when they will be staying with us. As you have seen, the dorm beds are three-quarter beds, so Toni and I can sleep in one and Jay can use the other one."

"And this is nothing unusual?"

"Not at all. If you leave Jay at home, you and Dad can use one bed and Toni and I will share the other."

"That definitely sounds like a plan," I teased.

"Can we get back to my request, please?" Jay said. "Would it be okay if I used your car for these occasional trips, Mom? I also need to investigate the university campus as I am considering applying to them for admission next year."

Crystal looked at me for input, and I nodded my head yes.

"How often would you be making these trips?" Crystal asked.

"Once or twice a month would be ideal, depending on conflicts. Toni is flying back to Puerto Rico for the Christmas break so who knows when we will be able to see each other if I cannot get down there now-and-then on weekends."

Crystal grinned. "I see. Are you okay with this, Toni?"

"Yes, Mrs. Tranter. I too would love to see Jay every few weeks throughout the school year."

"Okay, kids, we can make this work some weekends, then."

"Thanks, Mom. You're the greatest."

Jay-Jay made two visits to Charlotte and Toni before the girls started their Christmas exams. Toni returned to Puerto Rico for her Christmas break, and of course, Charlotte returned home to us. Jay's once or twice a month visits with the girls continued up until March break when Charlotte and Toni returned to our place for the week. Needless to say, Jay-Jay was ecstatic to have Toni around, around the clock. The two of them were now much more open concerning their affection for each other. At times we were perturbed that things were progressing too far too fast, but Crystal reminded me that two decades earlier we were not much different than these two now, only a bit older.

After March break, our world suddenly changed. Toni had previously been handed a local summer job posting by her biology professor, herself a native Puerto Rican, and she advised Toni to apply and use her for a reference. The job was in a research lab not far from the university and the wages she would receive from the employer were well over twice what she could make working in the hot fields in Puerto Rico for the summer, so she applied. She got the job. Toni was ecstatic. She was pretty sure her prof had inside connections to the lab but never asked and was never told. She was just thrilled to have the job in her desired field and get paid good money as well.

Along about the same time, Toni and Charlotte had been discussing their plans for the next school year and were not keen on applying to remain in residence. They located a furnished, two-bedroom rental unit close by and were seriously considering taking it. The hang-up was that it would be a one-year lease commencing after the spring classes finished. They wanted the apartment but were reluctant to grab it and pay for the summer months when they were not there. There was a reasonable chance that they could find some summer school students to sublet it for the summer months, but that was not guaranteed, so they held off on making a commitment until after they visited with us on March break.

The landscape suddenly changed when Toni received the summer job nearby. Charlotte had already accepted a summer job with the Promenade Parks & Recreation Department. Toni could afford her half of the rent but not Charlotte's half. The girls discussed their dilemma with Crystal and I while they were with us on their March break and we advised them if they really wanted the apartment then to go ahead and sign the lease, and we would cover Charlotte's portion of the rent, so the girls immediately signed the lease after their return to school.

The saga continues. Jay-Jay had requested admission to the girls' university along with some others, and his first acceptance was from the girls' university. He was so excited to be going there that he immediately accepted their offer of admission. That ticked me off considerably because there were a couple of other schools on his list that I felt offered a little better program in Astrophysics. We still are not done. The only summer job offer Jay had was for farm labor in the hot summer sun. He had done this the past two summers and had no desire to repeat that again. He discovered, with some research, that he could attend summer school and take two of his first-year university courses over the summer session which would free up his timetable in first year to include second-year courses that were follow-ups to the ones he completed over the summer. He insisted that by going to summer school each year he could knock a year off his normal program. Also, he argued that now that the girls would be signing their one-year lease he had no intention of applying for residence and would live with the girls in the apartment, so he might as well use it over the summer as I was paying for half of the rent anyway. I told him his mother and I would think about it.

I saw red, thinking of him and Toni alone in the apartment all summer, but Charlotte calmed me down when we managed to get her alone on one of Jay and Toni's last walks together before the girls departed. The apartment had a master bedroom and a smaller one. Each bedroom had twin beds which could be pushed together if a couple was in the room and they preferred it that way. She and Toni would take the master bedroom and have separate beds and Jay would get the smaller room.

"Is it safe to leave those two there all summer alone?"

"Toni is a virgin and has no plans on changing that status anytime soon. Mom confided to me a while back that you two deferred sex until after you were married. I am pretty sure that is also Toni's plan. Jay adores her and would never rape her. She will most likely be a virgin on her wedding night."

That private conversation calmed me down considerably, so I granted Jay's request to go to summer school and live with Toni in separate bedrooms.

Jay's plans worked out well. He received As in both of his summer school courses which gave him a head start over his classmates. Charlotte advised us that the apartment sharing with the three of them during the school year caused no problems whatsoever. The close relationship between Toni and Jay-Jay continued at a self-imposed, controlled pace.

The following year was effectively a carbon copy of the previous one. Toni worked at the lab again in the summer; Charlotte spent the summer with us and worked for the Parks & Recreation Department again, and Jay took two more summer school classes while living with Toni in their apartment before they were joined by Charlotte when the university year began.

This pattern pretty much repeated itself until graduations came upon them. With Jay's summer school credits, he managed to graduate the same year as the girls. What a marvelously proud day it was for Crystal and I, as well as Mom and Dad, to sit there in the sunshine and witness the three of them receive their diplomas! If that wasn't amazing enough, Jay-Jay topped it off later by showing us Toni's left hand with a lovely engagement ring on her finger. He had proposed to her the evening before. Of course, Toni accepted and Jay made Charlotte swear she would not spoil their surprise by telling us earlier. Definitely one of the happiest days of our lives.

Toni's parents, Juan and Maria Gonzales, flew up from Puerto Rico for the graduation ceremony. Really nice people. It was the first time we had an opportunity to meet them. The graduation ceremony was in September, not the spring when some are held, so Juan and Maria were able to spend a week with Toni and Jay-Jay in the rental apartment where they lived ever since the girls had moved out of the residence dorm. With Charlotte now graduated and beginning her teaching career, there was room for them to stay with our kids. Toni was working full time at the research lab now and Jay was working on his master's degree, so Juan and Maria had time throughout the day be check out the city at their leisure. Crystal and I, of course, needed to go back for school on Monday. Before we headed back to Mantle, I insisted on taking everyone out for a celebratory dinner at the kids' favorite restaurant.

30

At times, time flies. Toni and Jay got married a couple of months after their graduation. The little sneaks were married in a civil ceremony at the Mayor's office and said nothing about it to us family members until after the fact. Crystal and I speculated that Toni had likely managed to retain her virginity throughout all of the years they lived together, but one or both of them decided that this milestone needed to end. With Toni working full time and not having tuition expenses, she was able to help me pay for Jay's tuition and living expenses. They remained in that same apartment near the university until Jay finished his PhD in Astrophysics.

He was immediately snatched up by NASA and assigned to the Kennedy Space Center in Florida. Of course, Toni needed to leave her job back north. They settled in nearby Titusville. Toni was not able to find a full-time laboratory position close-by around the area so; after a couple of months of searching, the two of them decided it was a good time to start a family. Until she was eight months pregnant, Toni did work part-time in the lab at a cancer treatment facility in Titusville.

Consuelo Maria Tranter was born in August. Toni wanted to call her Consuelo, after her spirit guide who she was convinced was principally responsible for her and Jay-Jay suspecting that their souls indeed had preplanned, from the other side, for them to find each other in this life and eventually get married, just as we all heard from Consuelo in our living room that first time way back years before when Charlotte brought her dorm roommate home for Thanksgiving week. Later, after baby Consuelo arrived, Toni asked Consuelo the spirit guide if this was, in fact, preplanned before they incarnated. Her spirit guide confirmed that their souls definitely planned it this way but it was Toni and Jay's responsibility to figure it all out when on this side, so all she was permitted to do years earlier on Toni's first visit to our home was to drop that subtle hint that Jay-Jay picked right up on and doggedly ran with it. I am sure glad he did, as Crystal and I absolutely adore Toni. As an aside, I have no doubt that Crystal's and my souls preplanned our life together from the other side as well. Think about it, readers, could that have happened to you also?

The Maria portion of the name of this precious little bundle of joy was after Toni's mother. The baby was blessed with Toni's olive skin color and black hair, and eighteen years later, she was as gorgeous as her mother was when we first met Toni at age eighteen. We were definitely blessed all around.

Two years after the arrival of Consuelo, who we all began to call Connie as a baby, Robert Arthur Tranter made his screaming appearance. He pretty much took after Jay-Jay. Toni encouraged Jay to pick the names for his son. After two generations of Johns, Jay decided it was time for a change. The Robert is in honor of Jay's spirit guide Robbie, who Jay called Robert after he went off to university, and the Arthur was after my father. You can probably guess that we all called

Robert, the baby, Robbie after his arrival. I know I am probably a little biased, but he was definitely a handsome little fellow.

Time to catch up on our other offspring. After graduating with her degree in English and Theatre Arts, as well as a teaching certificate, Charlotte easily found a teaching opening in Theatre Arts, primarily, in a high school about the size of Promenade District High School, but a two-hour drive north of her university. It was a long drive from our home for Crystal and me, but we could do the round-trip in one very long day if necessary, whereas to visit Toni and Jay-Jay, driving or flying, was always a longer excursion.

Charlotte enjoyed lots of male company in high school and university, but Mr. Right apparently never made an appearance. In her new town, let's call it Sunshine, Charlotte quickly made friends with two other young ladies who, like her, were new to teaching. One of them, Delores, or Dolly Macomb, was a local girl who could teach physics and chemistry, so she had no difficulty snagging a position in her hometown high school after graduation. At some point early in Charlotte's first year at the school, Dolly introduced Charlotte to her older brother, Duncan, or Dunc, when the three of them happened to bump into each other one Saturday while out shopping. Dunc had a girlfriend at the time, but there was apparently an instant attraction between him and Charlotte.

A couple of months down the road, the now girlfriendless Dunc asked his sister if she would bring Charlotte over to his home for a barbeque. Dolly had a boyfriend at that time, so the four of them enjoyed an afternoon of chatting and dining, followed by an evening playing cards and board games. On a break from the games, Dunc put a CD of quiet dance music into his player and close body contact resulted. Charlotte told us later that the chemistry between her and Dunc was undeniable. Dunc asked her for a date the next Saturday and a budding romance quickly blossomed from that day on with Charlotte, Dunc, Dolly and her boyfriend Nick, spending a lot of time together. A year later, Dunc proposed to Charlotte and she happily accepted. They were married that summer.

The newlyweds waited a while, but as Charlotte approached the age of thirty, they decided it was family time. Donald Edward Macomb made his appearance a year later, followed by Rosemary, or Rosie Elizabeth joining the family eighteen months after her brother. Even though it was a long, one-day or even two-day trip, Crystal and I made it as often as we could and brought along Mom and Dad when they were game for long drives. The rules for maternity leaves were different at that time, at least in the Sunshine School District, than they had been thirty years earlier in the Promenade district when Crystal was birthing our wonderful offspring. Dunc was a successful dentist, and he encouraged Charlotte to leave her teaching position and start a second career as a mother. She loved her Theatre Arts classes and hated to walk away from them, but the arrival of Donnie quickly convinced her that a career as mother was the correct choice.

Crystal and I visited the four grandchildren as often as possible, of course, but the visits also ran both ways. Charlotte and Jay's families always visited us for at least a week during summer vacations and at times during the other school breaks where schedules could be coordinated. All of the grandchildren, who lived in towns or cities, loved their visits to our farm in the country where there were oodles of Mother Nature's treasures, and the old barn with our famous hayloft, to investigate. The sound of happy little voices enjoying the outdoors was heartwarming to us aging adults, trust me.

The years seemed to whiz by faster as we got older. Funny how that works. I mentioned way back that Crystal was six and a half years younger than me. She also was out of teaching for five years before our children started school. We did not think of it back then, and it probably would not have changed anything we did if we had thought about it back then, but because I had ten years more teaching experience than Crystal at the time I was eligible to retire on full pension way before she was even close. Fortunately, I did not have to retire, so I continued to teach past my retirement eligibility date as it made no great sense to me to go places, or sit around twiddling my thumbs, all by my lonesome. So, I just kept on teaching until Crystal was eligible for her pension also.

The landscape changed considerably over those years as we waited for Crystal to be able to retire. Dad passed away unexpectedly at seventy-eight and Mom joined him on the other side four years later. If I had of retired when eligible I would have been alone in our big old house all day.

Losing your parents is never easy, but as they come close to the magic eighty marker, we know their time clock is ticking down. It is the unexpected disasters that blast the stuffing out of us. It was the year that Crystal became eligible for her full pension and we were looking forward to a long and wonderful retiree's life. Dunc was in Cincinnati for a weekend dentists' convention in January. The weather had not been bad, but on his drive back to their home in Sunshine the rain turned to sleet. Apparently, a vehicle in the oncoming lane was going too fast for the deteriorating conditions and skidded over into Dunc's lane. Both drivers were dead by the time the emergency services vehicles arrived on the heart-breaking scene.

You are never prepared for a situation like this, trust me. It turned out that the other driver was drunk, so his insurance company denied all liability. He was living from paycheck to paycheck and had very little net worth, so a civil lawsuit was a waste of time. Dunc had mortgage insurance on their house which paid off Charlotte's remaining balance on her home.

Dunc also had a decent amount of life insurance,so money was available for Charlotte's needs for the short term. Dunc had worked in a large dental office in Sunshine, but he was not a part-owner. The family had lived well on his earnings over the years, but those earnings disappeared in one devastating second. Charlotte would need to find a good job before too long.

If there can be any good news in a terrible situation like this, it was the timing. Crystal and I planned to retire at the end of the school year. Promenade District High School would need two new English teachers. I was still the head of the English Department, so they would also need to appoint a new department head. Our principal was now a marvelous middle-aged woman named Eternity. Crystal and I spent a week with Charlotte and the children after the devastating accident, on a personal emergency leave from school, but when we returned to teaching duty we arranged for an after-school meeting with Eternity. Eternity arrived at our school after Charlotte graduated so the two had never met.

Charlotte's teaching resume was short but excellent, and the Theatre Arts designation on her teaching certificate was a definite bonus here. We needed an experienced Theatre Arts teacher. Before the meeting, Eternity was aware of Charlotte's personal loss and also that she was an experienced English and Theatre Arts teacher. She also knew that Crystal and I planned to retire but had not yet done so officially.

"Thank you for making the time to have this semi-personal chat with us," I started off.

"Anytime. I know you two well enough to know that you would not waste my time with trivialities. What's on your mind?"

"You know all about the unfortunate circumstances our daughter Charlotte has suddenly been thrust into recently. I would appreciate it if you would consider following a particular procedure in filling the two vacancies in the English department when Crystal and I retire."

"I'm listening. Please continue."

"I will retire first, probably tomorrow, effective the end of the school year. Crystal will not retire yet. I hope the board will allow you to post the vacant English headship position reasonably soon. I assume you and I will select the new English head, correct?"

"Yes."

"I know we must select the best candidate from the applications received. I also know that Abie will be applying for the position, and I doubt we will encounter anyone better qualified to fill the position than she is."

"You are likely correct there."

"Good. So, if we fill the headship internally, and Crystal later retires, then we will still need to hire two English classroom teachers from outside of the school. Am I correct that a three-person selection committee composed of you, I and the new English head will pick the two best candidates?"

Eternity grinned. "I see where you are going with this. You and Abie can outvote me on any candidate."

I chuckled. "I guess that would be correct unless you change the long-standing custom for selecting new teachers in a department. I will assure you that I will vote for the two best candidates who apply but if there are two close candidates for the second opening, I might just have to vote for my daughter who I know is an excellent candidate."

"That sounds fair. How long has Abie known your daughter?"

"All of her life."

Eternity erupted in hearty laughter. "You've got this all figured out, haven't you?"

"How about we use the term planned out?"

"Okay, I think we can follow your plan. You do know that

the Principal can overturn a vote if he or she does not think that the best candidates have been chosen?"

"Yes, but I assure you that if there are two much better candidates than our daughter, then I will vote for them over her."

"I believe you. Okay, we can go with your plan and hope that your daughter ranks as one of the top two candidates."

"Thank you, very, very much."

In the end, all of my plotting turned out to be unnecessary. Abie was the best candidate for the English headship vacancy and all three of us agreed that Charlotte was the top candidate for the vacant teaching positions. The second teacher we hired was Zackery, or Zack, Hunter. Like me, he had grown up in a rural area, and when he could not find a teaching job in a rural area, he took one in Cincinnati, again like me. Once more, like me, he was eager to get into a rural setting. Charlotte and Zack were clearly our best two choices, so the votes were unanimous on both counts. There is way more to Zack's story, but I will reveal it as it develops.

31

Once she knew that she was definitely moving out of Sunshine, Charlotte sprang into action. She worked diligently to declutter their home and spruce it up to near perfection so she could list it for sale. Dunc had dealt with most problems pretty promptly over the years, so very little serious work was required. Once listed, it sold in two weeks. Charlotte made sure the closing date was after the kids completed their school year. Before she started any serious packing, Charlotte went house hunting on the internet. She asked Crystal and me to check out some places in the Promenade and Mantle area for her that she considered a potential new home for her family. Nothing really struck her fancy, so as the closing date for her house sale loomed large on the horizon, I suggested she move her belongings into a storage locker in Promenade and settle in with Crystal and I until she discovered her ideal new home.

"Are you sure you want us to do that, Dad?"

"We raised you and your brother here in this house with the help of your grandparents, remember? You two didn't turn out too bad, well, at least you didn't."

Charlotte could not stop laughing. "Jay only has a PhD degree in Astrophysics. I'd say he didn't turn out too bad either."

"Oh, okay, I guess you're right. Seriously though, we would love to have you and the kids move in here for as long as you need to."

"You sure about that?"

"How many times do I have to tell you?"

"I guess that's enough. Okay, we will do that."

While Crystal and I were assisting Charlotte with her pending relocation, Abie ended up being Zack's go-to person. He knew absolutely nobody in our area except Abie, Eternity, and me, soon to be retired. He picked Abie, his new department head. He was recently divorced and living in a one-bedroom apartment in Cincinnati, we later learned, with a meager bank account thanks to the exorbitant spending of his ex-wife plus their costly divorce. He hoped to locate a decent apartment in the Promenade area and asked if Abie could check around our vicinity for him as he was too far away to do it efficiently. Abie and Rod, who was now the Chief of Police in Promenade, tracked down some contacts and asked them to check out the rental opportunities around here. Just like decades earlier when Crystal was looking for an apartment after she accepted our job offer at Promenade High, no descent apartments could be located.

Abie and Rod still lived in the same house in the country that she and her father bought and remodeled decades earlier. Their children were grown up, leaving them empty nesters. Abie, being one of the kindest people I have ever known, asked Rod if Zack could move in with them until he located an acceptable apartment. Rod agreed that it definitely made sense for the short term and Zack was overjoyed to accept their generous offer when they presented it to him.

I know I told you way back that the Obagatos, Radcliffs,

and we Tranters were all good friends. That did not change after our children grew up and flew the coop. We got together to play cards and have barbeques or dinners from time to time. Crystal and I decided that we could not leave Charlotte and the kids out of these get-togethers, and when we mentioned it to Abie, she figured she should also include Zack as well so when all were in attendance, we numbered ten.

Zack was out of his Cincinnati apartment and into Abie's home on July first, and Charlotte's gang joined us a couple of days later. For our Fourth of July celebration, Crystal and I put on a welcoming barbeque at our place. Fortunately, the weather cooperated quite nicely. As the evening began to cool off, Charlotte asked the kids if they wanted to go for a walk around the farm before bedtime. As always, their answer was of course. She then invited Zack to join them and he readily accepted, leaving us older folks to gab and enjoy our refreshments.

For decades, during our wonderful summer vacations, it was not unusual for Abie to pop over to our place once or twice a week, with kids when they were younger, or alone when they were older or out of the house, for no particular reason except to visit. Crystal and I would reciprocate as well. Now that we were retired there was no reason to stop this practice so Abie, with Zack as a sidekick as Rod was working, visited us regularly. By the time school was ready to begin for the new year, Charlotte and Zack were well acquainted and spent a lot of time outside playing or walking with Rosie and Donnie. Charlotte, Donnie, and Rosie all thought that Zack was a pretty neat guy. Actually, so did Crystal and I. It was easy to tell that he would be a wonderful addition to Promenade High.

The weeks of summer scooted by way too fast for the kids, and they were, at times, sad that they would no longer be seeing their old school chums. Charlotte tried to keep them as positive as she could by touting the opportunity for them to make a whole other bunch of new friends. When we were alone, Charlotte even admitted to us that she was also a bit apprehensive about starting her new career in a different school. I reminded her that I had switched to Promenade High after three years in Cincinnati with no difficulty and assured her that she was going to do just fine. A number of her teachers when she was a student at Promenade High were still there, I advised her, and that fact would help prevent her from feeling like a stranger. She also had Abie, her department head, as well as Zack to lean on, although I was certain that would not be necessary. I was right. Abie advised us at our next get-together that Charlotte and Zack fit right in with absolutely no problems.

As the school year rolled along, we all kept a lookout and an ear open for a new house for Charlotte and an apartment for Zack. None were discovered, so the status quo continued. One autumn evening after the kids were snuggled into bed and the three of us were chatting in the living room, Charlotte abruptly changed the topic of conversation.

"I know you two understand a lot more about souls and reincarnation than I do. With his sudden and unexpected passing, do you think that Dunc could be an earthbound spirit wandering around the vicinity of his accident, like the two spirits that Courtney helped to crossover many years ago? I talked to him a little bit about souls and reincarnation, and he met his Spirit Guide, but he never seemed to embrace the concept wholeheartedly."

"I guess his sudden passing makes him a candidate to be earthbound," I replied. "I gather you know the name of his Spirit Guide?"

"Yes."

"I suggest you ask Heather to appear to us and she should be able to help figure this out."

"Heather, please show yourself to us."

Heather materialized in the middle of the living room. "Hello, everyone."

"Did you hear the question I just asked my parents about whether Dunc's spirit might be earthbound after the way he died?"

"Yes. His spirit is not earthbound."

"Great. So, everything is fine with him, then?"

"Well, I'm not sure fine is exactly the proper description, either."

"I think we need an explanation."

"Understandable. As humans grow elderly, they become more aware of their pending departure from their current incarnation. Folks in their twenties and thirties give little or no thought to that possibility as they expect to be around for a number of more decades. When people like Duncan are suddenly and unexpectedly terminated from their human existence and thrust back into the spirit world, they are not very prepared for this sudden change of circumstances. Some do become earthbound, as you are aware, but others do cross-over yet are not prepared for this instant transition. They need to go through a period of acclimation to their new existence we sometimes refer to as conditioning. Duncan is going through this period of acclimation right now."

"How long does this take?"

"Until the acclimation is completed. Remember though, time in the spirit world does not exist."

"Where is Duncan's spirit guide, Marco?"

"He is with Duncan still, helping his soul through this acclimation process."

"Is there anything I can do to help?"

"Not really. You have already done your part by introducing him to his spirit guide and the existence of souls and reincarnation. Consider how much more difficult this unexpected transition might be for any human who does not have any knowledge of these subjects. You now must get on with your life and stop worrying about him. His soul will be fine, and you will meet again in the future, as I'm sure you know."

"We are all in the same soul group?"

"Yes, we are all in the same soul group."

In February, after he knew Charlotte had been a widow for over one year, Zack somewhat sheepishly asked Charlotte if it would be okay if they began dating. She was taken by surprise at first, but after she had time to think about it, she realized that they were quite compatible and always got along wonderfully. She originally asked him for a week to think about it and then discussed it with Crystal and me. We told her we really liked Zack and emphasized that she was still young enough to start a new life and also that there was no reason to spend the rest of her life as a widow. The next day after school she advised Zack that they could start dating but she needed to take things very slowly. He said of course that was fine.

By the end of the school year, Zack was spending more time at our house with Charlotte and the boys than he was with Abie and Rod. I should clarify that. I am talking about awake time only. There were no sleepovers at our house, at least when we were home and not off gallivanting and enjoying our long-awaited retirement. I also want to add that Abie never said anything about Zack not being at her house on any mornings. That's all I know.

In July, Zack upped the ante on their relationship with what I can only describe as an open-ended proposal of marriage. He told Charlotte that he hoped that she would someday agree to marry him and bear him at least one child. He told her to take all of the time she wanted to think about it, emphasizing that there was no time limit for her to respond but to let him know whenever she was certain of her decision. She assured him that she would give his proposal careful consideration but not to expect a quick answer. He was happy with this response. Charlotte asked Crystal and I for our opinion on the situation, and we assured her that we would be thrilled to see her married to Zack but that she needed to make her decision from the heart. She thanked us for our advice.

Donnie was eight at the time and Rosie had recently turned seven. Charlotte worked diligently at quizzing them about their feelings for Zack and carefully attempting to create the understanding that their father would never be returning home to them. After quizzing them a number of times on whether they liked spending time with Zack, which both confirmed they did, she eventually added during these little chats that Zack would like to be their new daddy and asked if that would be okay with them. They really had never given any thought to that possibility at their tender ages, so her question took them by surprise. Donnie asked what Daddy would think about that. Charlotte may have anticipated this question or was simply a quick thinker but her response was, *Daddy cannot come back and be with us ever again, and I think he would not want you to grow up without a daddy so I am pretty sure he would think Zack was a pretty good stand-in or replacement for him.*

That evening we were allowed to listen in when Charlotte telephoned Zack.

"Hello."

"Yes."

"Hi. Yes, what?"

"Oh, my," she could not resist teasing him. "Here you have already forgotten that little open proposal you made to me a few weeks ago. I guess I will need to reconsider my response."

"No! No! No! No! Don't do that. I accept your original yes. You just caught me by surprise when I was not thinking about it. I love you with all of my heart, and I can't wait to marry you. How about tomorrow?"

"What! I can't be ready that quick."

"Sure you can. You had one big wedding and so did I. I am happy with a wedding at the mayor's office as soon as possible. Are you game?"

Charlotte thought about that for a few moments. "That would save us a lot of money, that's for sure. Are you sure you would be happy with it?"

"I want to marry you anywhere, anytime, even jumping out of an airplane with parachutes."

"That's a definite no."

"Just teasing. Shall we visit the mayor tomorrow morning and see when we can set this up?"

"I'll meet you there at nine. I love you."

"Deal. And I love you more."

"Get a good night's sleep now."

"Not a chance. I'll be thinking of you all night."

"I should hope so. Bye," she said and quickly hung up the phone.

I just sat back and enjoyed watching Crystal and Charlotte sob on each other's shoulder. I will admit my eyes were also rather bloodshot at the time.

32

The betrothed couple obtained their marriage license before nine-thirty the next morning, then picked out and purchased their rings immediately thereafter. Zack brought a nice suit from home that he could wear, and Crystal insisted she was buying Charlotte a new dress for this memorable occasion. The girls took off to the classiest dress shop in Promenade and were fortunate to find a stunning peach-colored dress that fit Charlotte perfectly for the occasion. Abie rode to town with Zack and went searching for Rod to bring him up to date on the proceedings while Zack and I tried to keep Donnie and Rosie under control as they excitedly waited for the imminent event scheduled for one o'clock at city hall. Donnie was the best man and ring bearer while Rosie was the flower girl. Crystal and I, along with Abie and the Chief of Police in his uniform, were the thrilled witnesses. I took the entire entourage out for lunch after the ceremony. All of the other relatives on both sides were located too far away to make the ceremony on short notice, so they were updated on the wondrous event, after the fact.

Abie had a sneaky plan, and she managed to reveal it to Crystal in secret sometime through the assorted activities. Crystal thought it was a wonderful idea. Abie and Rod spent the night in Charlotte's bed so the newlyweds could be alone at Abie and Rod's home to make as much noise as they wanted. We were never shared any details, of course, but they both looked rather tired the next day. I was actually pretty thrilled about that after the heartbreak Charlotte went through losing Dunc and the frustrations Zack experienced throughout his divorce wars with his ex.

At our wedding luncheon, I told the happy newlyweds that I would take care of a surprise honeymoon vacation for them and asked for three preferences from each of them. The only common preference was Hawaii, so I booked them a weeks' vacation in a ritzy hotel in early August before the new school year started. Thankfully, they had a wonderful time.

Back to reality. Zack moved out of Abie's home and into Charlotte's bedroom the day after the wedding, of course. They continued to look for a nice house they liked or, if necessary, a large apartment, to move into. Nothing they really liked appeared on the scene. The longer they remained in our house, the more I realized how similar their situation was to when Crystal and I raised our family in my parents' house. Of course, Charlotte was perfectly familiar with all of the advantages of that arrangement throughout her first eighteen years, but this concept was totally foreign to Zack. After a while when Zack became accustomed to having resident kid-sitters available day or night, most of the time, he began to realize that this type of arrangement wasn't such a bad idea after all.

Two years later, after she worked on Zack for who knows how long, Charlotte hit Crystal and me with a proposal. She had all of the money, from the sale of her house in Sunshine, stashed away in safe investments. She was aware that approximately fifty years earlier I temporarily died twice on the hospital's operating table after the horrific automobile accident in my first year of college in Cincinnati. She also knew that when I received my accident settlement, I paid off my parents' mortgage. We did not have a mortgage to pay off, but she insisted that she and Zack wanted to buy our house instead of looking around any longer for a different home. The only condition, she added, was that we agree to continue to live with them for the rest of our days. I asked for a little time for us to consider this unexpected development and Charlotte told us to take all of the time we needed as she had no intention of revoking the offer.

Crystal and I talked about it for a few days, but I always knew in my heart it would take place. We loved raising our children with the help of my parents and we agreed we would love to help raise our grandchildren as well. After we said yes to Charlotte's offer, she got a Promenade lawyer, who she actually went to school with and even dated for a while as a teenager, to take care of the necessary paperwork. With that nicely out of the way, she hit us with one more surprise, sort of. She told us she and Zack decided they would like a child, or maybe two, soon. She also advised us that she would not hold us to our promise to not move out on them because at the time we agreed to it all of us were only thinking two youngsters running around and not four. Crystal and I looked at each other. "We're in. Go make some babies," Crystal replied.

Morgan Edward Hunter arrived a year later followed by Faith Melody Hunter two years after her brother. Crystal and I loved it, maybe except for a few long days when they were screaming too much, but we still had no doubts that the plusses far outnumbered the minuses. The old procedures for requesting leaves from the school board had not changed from the time that Crystal and Abie had to deal with them.

Charlotte, with our approval, took a different approach. She took a one-year leave around the birth of Morgan and then went back to teaching for a year. Pregnant with Faith, Charlotte was then able to take two years leave without resigning her position. Crystal and I liked the way she planned that all out.

Having four kids in the house at our age was not a piece of cake, but when the racket sometimes got us down, we would remind each other how lucky we were to be able to share the growing-up years of at least four of our six grandchildren. I did not plan it that way, but I definitely would not have changed it if I could have. The saddest part was that we never saw nearly enough of Jay and Toni's youngsters in Florida. Can't win them all, I guess.

Now, before you feel sorry for us because we were stuck at home for much of our retirement years, you need to remember that Charlotte and Zack were both teachers with over three months of vacation time in every calendar year. That meant Crystal and I could take off on vacations every summer and sometimes even during the shorter breaks like Christmas and March break. And we did. I am pretty sure that we actually got away for at least one week, and often more, every summer vacation except the year Charlotte and the kids moved in and the summer she and Zack got married. That is a damn nice vacation record if I have to say so myself. We visited Paris, London, Australia, Japan, Hawaii, the Cayman Islands, Portugal and Spain, Barbados, and numerous other exciting destinations. We definitely were not housebound grandparents.

If you are parents, you will know how fast the years sail by as your children grow up way too quickly. That also applies for grandparents, take my word for it. Before we knew it, Donnie, now insisting he be called Don, and Rosie were attending the high school where mom and dad taught, and

Morgan and Faith were into elementary school. Then, seemingly like the blink of an eye, Don and Rosie were off to college with Morgan and Faith joining their parents at Promenade District High School. Where does the time go?

Once all four grandchildren were off to school, Crystal and I enjoyed more us time. Crystal wanted to and did most of the cooking for our family of eight throughout the week, and Charlotte would banish her from the kitchen on weekends. If we were barbequing, I handled the responsibilities throughout the week and Zack laid me off on weekends. Everyone seemed to be quite happy with that arrangement. During school vacations this system often got thrown out the window as sometimes we had company or Crystal and I, and at other times Charlotte and Zack, with or without children, were enjoying a holiday vacation.

With everyone in school except Crystal and I, we had unlimited opportunities to visit with our Spirit Guides, Courtney and Tom. Yep, they were still around. Tom referred to them as lifers as we were stuck with them for life whether we liked it or not. Even though we would tease them at times just to get them riled up, we were thrilled to have discovered them as youngsters and become educated by them throughout our lives on life on the other side.

I also used all of this free time to start writing this story. I know I mentioned way back that I should have started it years before, but I never seemed to get around to it. I'll use the excuse, and there is certainly a lot of truth to it, that back in the earlier years I did not have the free time that I have now as first the children and later the grandchildren kept us hopping. Now, Don and Rosie have graduated from college and are pursuing their chosen careers. Don has followed the family tradition and become an English teacher. He snatched his first teaching position in Lexington as, like me and Zack, he was not offered one in a desired, more rural setting. Rosie is a nurse and is currently working at a hospital in Lakeland, Florida. With Toni and Jay-Jay still living in Florida, it gives Crystal and I a good excuse to enjoy the life of snowbirds and spend the colder months close to them and Rosie.

Morgan and Faith are both in college now, and I will fill you in on their escapades when they graduate and get settled into a career.

Hi, this is Crystal.

My beloved John passed away quietly in his sleep a month ago, as I am writing this, at the age of eighty-two. I knew he was writing his story, actually our story, and many times, he would ask me to confirm whether his memories of our past were correct or not. Usually he was right, but a few times I was able to add to or clarify his remembrances. I do not know why, and I never would ask, but he never invited me to actually read the uncompleted manuscript. I would never snoop into something he seemed to wish to remain personal. And I did not. I came across it as Charlotte and I were working on cleaning out some of his clothing and other possessions, and finally read it. I was impressed at how well he recorded our story and I asked Charlotte and then Zack to read it also. We all agreed that it needed to be shared with the world. A boyhood friend of Zack's is an author and he put me in touch with his publisher. The publisher asked for the manuscript, so we sent it to him. I hope he likes it as much as we do.

Crystal

Dear reader,

We hope you enjoyed reading *The Door To Forever*. Please take a moment to leave a review in Amazon, even if it's a short one. Your opinion is important to us.

Discover more books by Doug Simpson at https://www. nextchapter.pub/authors/doug-simpson

Want to know when one of our books is free or discounted for Kindle? Join the newsletter at http://eepurl.com/bqqB3H

Best regards,

Doug Simpson and the Next Chapter Team

You might also like

Glorious Incorporated by Steven Neil Moore

To read the first chapter for free go to:
https://www.nextchapter.pub/books/glorious-incorporated

Printed in Great Britain
by Amazon